Milkweed

Milkweed

Larah Peterson

Ivy
House
Publishing Group
United States of America

PUBLISHED BY IVY HOUSE PUBLISHING GROUP
An Imprint of Pentland Press, Inc.
5122 Bur Oak Circle, Raleigh, NC 27612
United States of America
919-782-0281

ISBN 1-57197-305-2
Library of Congress Control Number: 2001 135707

Printed in the United States of America

This book is dedicated to my mother,
Alice Wheaton Peterson,
who taught me the meaning, appreciation,
and secrets of life.

TABLE OF CONTENTS

Chapter 1
Spring Promise

As she wandered down the dirt road, she kicked at a stone and diligently kept it on an even course in front of her. If only her life could be so easily kept on track. Ah, but this was not the time to nurture regrets. Now was the time to look forward and make plans for a bright future. Holly Cummings felt that things would go her way if she just kept a true course.

Coming from a dirt-poor farm in South Carolina, she knew how to keep her chin up and remain strong. Lord knows Ma and Pa had tried to do their best, but life was hard, and some of the seven kids had been sickly. There was never enough time or extras to keep a young child feeling warm and loved.

Her mother, Elizabeth Barkley, had met and married her young husband at the age of sixteen, when he came east for a summer vacation visit to the town of Cotton Grove, from a small town west of there called Prairie Ridge. That was in Piedmont Plateau, the lower range of foothills of the Blue Ridge Mountains, in the central western part of the state.

He had arrived in Cotton Grove at the end of May to stay for the summer with his Aunt Reba and Uncle Hank, helping on the farm with their three kids in picking the peaches for preserves. By the beginning of July, Elizabeth knew that Jed Cummings was the only man she would ever love, and he felt the same way about her. She had the bluest eyes, and her sweet smile just melted his heart from the first time he saw her at his cousin Jethro's house. "She understands my feelins 'bout so many things and never makes me feel awkward like other girls do," Jed thought.

Jed was a tall boy with clear brown eyes and a strong pair of shoulders, just made for farming and tending the earth in the manner that was held dear by the folk in the hills of western South Carolina.

Milkweed

"Just come over here and start pickin' these peaches, Jed," said Hank Perkins. "You can join Elizabeth and Sally and Peter. We'll get the job done in half the time with your help."

Elizabeth was secretly happy to have him there near her. She had thought he would have to go off and tend the horses and goats with the other boys. The hot sun burned down on their shoulders, and even the caps that they wore didn't shade their faces from the glare. The perspiration rolled down Jed's face, showing the fine bones that he had inherited from his mother's side of the family.

His dark brown shock of hair fell across his forehead, and he pushed it back frequently, partly from the sticky heat and partly from self-consciousness in front of Elizabeth. Jed worked extra hard picking the peaches to please his uncle and to impress Elizabeth that he was certainly an older young man. After all, he had just celebrated his seventeenth birthday. She was only sixteen, and he felt mature and capable, eager to show her he knew his way around.

Cousin Jethro thought the whole scene was a waste of time. He had no time for girls, and Elizabeth was his sister's friend, not in the same league with other girls. "Jus' let me go huntin' with my houn' dog for raccoons," he said. He was happy tending to the animals and being with the other boys.

After the day's work was done, they would rush into the house to wash their hands and faces from the sweat and dust of the day and sit at the kitchen table for some homemade lemonade and cookies. Aunt Reba made the best oatmeal cookies in the whole county.

"You kids are doin' a top-notch job out there. We'll have 'nough peaches picked to supply Standard Brands with a full quota of peach jam for the summer production time." Aunt Reba was proud. "Maybe this year we'll make 'nough extra to catch up from last year's shortage."

Jed looked at Elizabeth, admiring her even though she was dusty and exhausted from the day's hard labor. She sensed his approval and smiled shyly back, hoping that no one noticed.

Working together like this gave them a sense of togetherness, giving them a strong bond, which they would always appreciate.

Later, it was time for Elizabeth to return to her own home and help her mother get the younger ones ready for bed. Jed and Jethro offered to walk her down the dirt road that lead to her small farmhouse. It was weathered clapboard, needing paint badly, like the hand of an old sailor who had been at the helm of his ship for too many years, where the sun had baked the life out of it. The small yard in front hadn't seen any care in a long time. The few chickens that wandered around from the back scratched in the dirt to see what was interesting to peck at. There was not a flower or green bush in the yard, just bare dirt and two scraggly trees. There was no time for frivolous chores here, just the many necessary ones to keep the family going.

"Elizabeth, where have you been so late?" called her mother. "I need your help, girl."

Elizabeth felt the hot rush come over her face as she looked away from Jed in embarrassment.

"Who's this boy, I never laid eyes on him 'afore?"

"Ma, this is Jethro's cousin, Jed. He's from Prairie Ridge, over to the east. He's here for the summer to help with the harvestin'."

"Well, that's all fine and dandy, now, but I need help here with these young-uns."

With that, Elizabeth reluctantly went into the small house to ready the little ones for bed. She stole glances at Jed and Jethro as they walked back down the dusty road toward home.

The milkweed pods in the fields around them were standing tall and straight. The pods were swollen with their seeds, attached to fluffy parachutes, ready to take flight with the next breeze to follow nature's plan.

Elizabeth felt as light as the milkweed seeds since she had first met Jed. She felt ready to take flight, too. She didn't care where she came down to earth.

Chapter 2
Autumn Beginnings

Elizabeth and Jed had worked especially hard that day, and felt exhausted in the hot August sun.

"Let's take a break and go for a swim in the creek down the south meadow," Jed suggested. "I need to cool off."

"Right. I can't work any more until *I* cool off."

The two skipped away down the road while the others went to get some lemonade and take a break. Jed took off his shirt and jumped into the cool stream, staying under the water for as long as he could. When he broke the surface, he saw Elizabeth treading water near him with only her undergarments on. She had placed her shirt, shorts, and shoes in a neat pile at the roots of the big oak tree. Jed swam up to her, giving her a big hug and pushing her under the cool water's surface.

"Yeow!" she gasped. "Not fair!"

With that she shoved him under, and he choked on the mouthful of water that he didn't have time to avoid taking in. They frolicked in the cool clean water for a few minutes, then climbed up the bank to the shade of the oak tree. He put his arm around her, and pulled her to him, giving her a strong embrace and kiss.

"I want to marry you, Elizabeth, you are my best friend and the most wonderful girl in the world! Let's not wait another day. We can have a wonderful life together, raise some kids, and have our own piece of land. I can leave school now, I have finished all but the last year, and I think I have learned all I need to from books and stuff. Whatever else I need to learn, I can get while I work my land. My dad always promised me the lower twenty-five acres to work as my own when I settled down. You'll like Prairie Ridge, Elizabeth. Folks there are real friendly and helpful. What do you say? Let's do it!"

Milkweed

Elizabeth paused. She didn't know what to say. This was so sudden, but the most wonderful idea she could imagine . . . life together with Jed . . . on their own . . . what could be better? Tears welled up in her eyes.

She caught her breath and said, "Jed, I'll love you forever, we'll get married tomorrow!"

Jed replied, "All we have to do is go to City Hall and they'll do it there. Jethro will stand up for us."

That evening, everyone sat around the back porch drinking lemonade and trading tall tales. Sally Perkins, Jethro's sister and a year younger than Elizabeth, was reliving her past school year, and all the exciting adventures that a fifteen-year-old has to tell. Sally was very outgoing and well liked by her friends because of her bouncy blonde curls and easy manner. Jethro, on the other hand, was quieter and did not care to socialize as much, preferring to go off and hunt with his dog, Blue.

It was hard bringing up the subject of marriage with Jethro, but Jed waited until just the right moment when everyone was starting to split up for the night.

"Jethro, would you come with me while I walk Elizabeth home? I have a question to ask you."

Jethro suspected nothing. "Sure, Jed, what's going on?"

As they rounded the bend in the narrow dirt road, Jethro began to feel suspicious, noticing the secret smiles that were transpiring between Jed and Elizabeth.

"Say, tell me now, you two. What's up?"

"Well Jed, I'm sure you know how I feel about Elizabeth, and she feels the same about me. We're going to City Hall tomorrow to get married!"

"What?" cried Jethro. "Are you crazy? You're both too young."

"No, we're not. We know what we want. We're going back to Prairie Ridge and settle down on the land that Pa promised me. Elizabeth doesn't have any future here, just helping out at home and watching the world go by."

"But—" Jethro knew it was no use.

"But nothin'. It's been decided. I'm countin' on you to stand up for us."

Jethro gave in to his older cousin's determination. He knew that he could sneak off for an hour or two in the morning to accompany them to City Hall without anyone knowing about it.

Early the next morning, Elizabeth packed up her favorite church dress and a delicate pearl and gold link necklace she had gotten several years ago with some money she had diligently saved over the years. She left the house and her family for the last time in her life. She didn't suspect that she would never see them again. She wrote a note, which she planned to give to Jethro to take to them after she and Jed were well on their way.

Jed was waiting around the bend of the narrow dirt road on which she lived. He had arrived a bit early. He was eagerly anticipating the day and making sure that Elizabeth became his wife. He envisioned a future for them that was full with the happiness of children of their own and a life enriched from the farming he had grown up with.

Jethro was also waiting at the crossroads, where the road on which he lived intersected the lane that went to Elizabeth's home. Jethro was quiet and a little reluctant, thinking that his cousin was making a mistake in assuming this responsibility when he was still so young. Jethro was aware that his parents had not had an easy time bringing up their three children and running the small farm, which required long hours and hard, physical work. He said nothing, though, feeling that they would not listen, anyway. His cousin Jed was older by only one year, but so much more settled and wanted a different type of life than Jethro envisioned for himself.

The trio walked the four miles into town and arrived at the steps of City Hall shortly after it had opened. They walked through the large oak and glass double doors of the old building, feeling a bit nervous, but optimistic and eager.

The woman at the first window greeted them with a cheery smile and asked if she could help them. Jed took control and announced that he and Elizabeth were there to get married in a civil ceremony with Jethro as their witness. The woman smiled and asked if they could show birth certificates. Jed had his, as he always carried a copy of it around in his wallet, ever since he first got a job when he was fourteen. Elizabeth had a copy of hers taken from the town register.

She then excused herself and went into the washroom to put on her best dress and pearl and gold necklace. When she emerged, Jed was speechless at seeing his lovely young bride looking so radiant and elegant. Elizabeth could see the happiness and pride in his eyes, and she felt like she never had before.

Then they proceeded to the next window where an older gentleman sat with two plaques on display proclaiming him a Justice and Notary Public. He beckoned them to step inside and into a small chamber at the back of the office. He positioned them side by side in front of him with Jethro standing to Jed's side. They had no rings, but the justice let them use one that couples in this situation used, and they were happy with this.

The justice read the wedding vows to them, and Jethro seemed to get into the mood of the moment and actually seemed proud to be a part of it. Jed and Elizabeth each had a glow about them and exchanged their vows with emotion and a promise for the future.

Chapter 3
Harvest Dedication

As Jed and Elizabeth returned to Prairie Ridge, Jed's parents, Billy Joe and Selma Cummings, were struggling to keep control of their modestly sized farm. The mortgage had been refinanced three different times over the last ten years, without the increase in crops that Billy Joe and Selma had longed for.

The summers over the last three years had been unusually dry, and the depleted soil could no longer provide a rich crop like it had in earlier years. The local bank had been most accommodating, but now they were obligated to call the note on the property. Billy Joe had been able to separate the lower twenty-five acres that he had promised to Jed before the note was called in, but Jed and Elizabeth had to build a home and get things in line to begin their plan for the future.

Times were starting to look difficult with Jed's parents living with them. Billy Joe was helpful in building the small three-room bungalow that they all occupied. The front room was for sitting, after chores were done and because of the shortage of space, Jed and Elizabeth had to have their handmade bed there, too. The kitchen was large enough for a cast-iron cookstove and benches and a table. The other room was the bedroom for Billy Joe and Selma. It took Jed and Billy Joe two months to complete the bungalow using logs cut from the woods nearby. Jed was pretty proud of it, but it would have been nice if he and Elizabeth could have had it to themselves.

The first spring planting started normally.

"Elizabeth, all we need now is to just finish planting these cotton seeds before the rains start. The plowing is finished, thank God, if we can just get a break."

Jed was able to trade some labor in the fields for his neighbor five miles down the road for an old horse and single furrow plow. He and Elizabeth and Billy Joe took turns working the plow and horse. It was strenuous labor, out in the hot sun for six and seven hours at a time.

Elizabeth felt like she had aged a lot in a short time. Selma was not able to help because of her heart palpitations, which came all too frequently. However, she made hearty but plain meals for them out of beans, leftover crops of soybeans and so forth, that the general store offered to those most needy. Sometimes she was able to get a piece of meat to put into the stews to add tastiness and substance.

Elizabeth had not been feeling very well for the past four or six weeks, and she blamed it on the strenuous schedule that they all kept. Being out in the hot sun and working so hard made her feel nauseous and weak. She kept going, though, because she and Jed had a dream, and all they had to do was work a little longer and keep going, then things would work out.

This morning when she awoke she felt different. Her stomach had really swelled up and she had a creeping feeling that she might be having a baby. "Gosh," she thought, "I am only sixteen and a half years old. I wish we could have had a couple more years to get ahead before we start a family. One more mouth to feed would make it harder." Also, she would not be able to work as hard later on. "I won't say anything to Jed," she thought. "He has enough on his mind with the planting." It was not easy to hide her changing shape, though. She had been a slim girl and the extra pounds and swollen waistline were obvious. Finally, after the fourth month of her condition, Jed spoke up.

"I see a change in my beautiful wife. Are we going to begin our family soon?"

"Jed is always so thoughtful and caring," thought Elizabeth. "He just doesn't see any difficulties coming our way. I envy his optimism."

The planting started out on schedule; however, spring rains came early, and they had to work feverishly to get the last acres of cotton planted. Working in the pouring rain dampened their spirits and exhausted them. Elizabeth felt it the most, as she had become unusually large and short of breath as the months went on.

The first acres planted took hold in the rich soil of the South Carolina farmland, and they could see the young plants struggle to shoot through the earth to absorb the sun. The last acres did not do well, though, because the rainfall had washed the young roots out before they could get a hold.

"I guess our crop will be a smaller one, Pop. We'll have to cut back on expenses to make anything this year." Billy Joe didn't want to give in to the hardship of cultivating crops on the Piedmont Plateau, but he knew they would be in for a rough year.

The summer months passed without incident, Elizabeth celebrated her seventeenth birthday and Selma tried to make it festive by decorating a small biscuit-like cake she had baked and garnished with fresh strawberries.

Elizabeth was quite large by now, and everyone suspected she might be having twins by her size. She felt very uncomfortable, but never said a word to Jed because he was so conscientious about the farm and providing for them all. Elizabeth thought to herself, "I feel like those milkweed plants—ready to split wide open I have grown so big."

Elizabeth kept up her work schedule. Picking time was beginning, and they needed everyone to pitch in so the cotton would not dry out on the stem. Even Selma spent three or four hours a day picking all she could, and lugging the heavy canvas bags of freshly picked cotton over to the loading area to be brought to the cleaning machines at the mill. Before the bags were taken they were weighed and the fair price was calculated for the growers. There was a narrow window of harvest time; if that was missed the cotton would be too dry to be worth much.

Elizabeth was out in the field early one morning picking the cotton and hauling it for loading when she felt a sharp pain stab through her abdomen and continue around her back. She let out a cry and gasped for breath. No one heard her because they were all out of earshot, concentrating on the cotton plants.

Elizabeth crumpled to her knees and stayed there for a few minutes until the pain subsided. Then she crawled to her feet and started for the area she knew Jed would be near. She felt another sharp pain and fell again. She called out for him, sweat pouring down her face, and prayed he would hear. Minutes went by as she lay there and two more pains came, each time taking her breath away.

Finally, she heard Jed say, "Elizabeth, honey, I thought I heard you. Are you all right? Is it the babies?"

"Yes, Jed, they're comin'. Help me get to the house! Your ma can help me there."

"Hold on, now, I'll get you there." Jed picked her up in his strong arms and carried her all the way to the house.

There, Selma settled her on the double bed that she and Jed shared and got a bucket of hot water to assist in the births. Sure enough, within a half-hour the first little Cummings made her debut. It was a baby girl weighing six pounds and giving a good loud wail to let everyone know she was here. Three minutes later another little girl arrived, weighing five pounds and only giving a soft whimper.

Elizabeth felt the pride of motherhood swell over her, and the relief of knowing that her ordeal was over. She sank into a deep sleep as Selma wrapped the girls in soft cotton and settled them in the handmade cradles Jed had carved for his babies.

After Elizabeth awoke, she wanted to hold the girls and enjoy them, and make sure they were all right. She examined the first one. "She reminds me of Jed, with her beautiful bones and thick chestnut hair. I know it's August, not Christmas, but I'll call her Holly."

The second girl was a little smaller and quieter. She had Elizabeth's blue eyes and sweet face, and Elizabeth decided to call her Anna. Jed came in and exclaimed over the twin girls, hugging Elizabeth and feeling so blessed with his babies.

Chapter 4
Winter's Struggle

By October, the difference between little Holly and Anna was noticeable. Holly was growing, with a good appetite and happy smile. Anna, however, was smaller and didn't eat as well. She was a good baby, but quiet and seemed more fragile.

The harvesting of the cotton went well, but the quantity of good cotton to sell to the mill was down, and the small family had to make do with less than expected. As winter neared and the weather was colder, Anna became sick, and needed attention around the clock because of coughing and influenza that wouldn't go away.

Elizabeth was up at night and felt tired most days from the two infants. Selma helped as much as she could, but Elizabeth was nursing, and if she wasn't feeding one, she was feeding the other. Jed used this time to make repairs around the farm. He mended fences and helped harvest fall vegetables that they needed for the winter.

In February, Elizabeth realized that she probably was going to have another baby and this was not good news to the struggling parents, but they both hoped for a boy this time and felt that it was God's will, so everything would be all right. The winter passed, and spring came quickly, and it was time for planting again. Elizabeth could not work too much in the fields with the two little girls to tend to, but she did as much as she could, letting Selma watch them for a few hours at a time. Selma could not carry them around much because of her shortness of breath, but she enjoyed her granddaughters immensely. As summer advanced, Elizabeth became more uncomfortable, and the humid weather bothered her.

In September, she gave birth to Andrew Lee, named for the Civil War general Andrew Jackson. The little boy was welcomed into the family, and they called him Andy. The twin girls were a year old and thought the baby brother quite interesting.

Jed maintained his gentle, optimistic manner and loved his family deeply.

Over the next five years, Elizabeth gave birth to three more children, two boys and a girl.

The small house became very crowded, and Jed and Billy Joe built another small room onto the house so the children could sleep in there, and Elizabeth and Jed kept the smallest baby with them.

Holly was a tremendous help to her mother, being strong and smart as well. Anna had always struggled with her health and was sweet, but not able to do much to help. The twin girls were seven now and in school as much as possible except for harvest time. Elizabeth was glad she had Selma to help her with her large brood of children—six was a lot to take care of, especially when one was sick. Little Anna never did develop much resistance, but kept going along with the happy outlook of her father.

By the end of the harvest season that year, Selma was obviously losing ground in her struggle with her heart condition. She was in bed most of the days, and when she did get up, she was very weakened and short of breath. She passed away the last week in November, and everyone in the valiant family felt a great loss because of the kindness and helpful ways she had always exhibited in spite of her poor health. Billy Joe was devastated. He and Selma had shared their lives since they were teenagers. It was hard to imagine life without her.

It was good that he lived with Jed and Elizabeth and was involved in all the activity and work of their farm life. Holly and Anna were now ten years old, and Holly felt more responsibility for the younger children now that her grandmother was gone and her mother needed so much help.

The work never ceased; if it wasn't the cotton crop, it was the cooking, or the cleaning, laundry, or caring for the younger ones. Holly had to grow up fast, and sometimes she felt slightly put upon, but then she felt how lucky she was compared to Anna, who had to miss out on so much because of her illnesses. Holly had the strength and perseverance of the milkweed plant, just as her mother did. She was bright and endured with grace and fortitude, but inside she was soft and delicate, as were the milkweed seeds with their downy softness and ability to float above the troubles of the world.

The four younger ones helped with the crops and work around the house as much as they could, but still there was so much work and never enough money to take care of good food or a new piece of clothing once in a while. All their clothes had to be mended over and over again until there was nothing left to work with.

Holly made all her clothes from scraps of fabric that she got from the general store on sale or left over from bolts of fabric that were discontinued. She learned how to tailor clothes to fit correctly and sew the seams to allow the fabric to fall nicely, and show the clothes to their best advantage. All of the cloth that she worked with was used with good taste that she seemed to come by naturally. Holly only chose conservative fabrics, of neutral colors, some dark, some brighter, but always appealing to the eye and seeming to stay in style.

Chapter 5
Work Ethic

When Holly was fifteen, the owner of the general store, Bill Talbot, offered her a part-time position as Girl Friday for him to help with any necessary chores around the store or demands that he might have to deal with. She was fast and accurate when figuring out the customer's bills and courteous, with an innate talent for dealing with people. Talbot was most appreciative of Holly's contribution and felt that his business had grown within two months of Holly's starting to work for him.

"Holly," Bill said one Friday afternoon in October, "I need to go up to Greenville to visit my sister, who is in the hospital. I am the only family she has, and I will be gone until Sunday around dinnertime. Do you think you could run the store by yourself?"

"Why, certainly, Mr. Talbot. I feel right at home, and I know I can handle whatever comes up. You go and don't give it another thought."

"I knew I could count on you. I'll see you on Sunday around five."

Being in the store alone was a great treat for Holly. She really liked having the responsibility and control of what went on. She opened up as usual on Saturday morning at 7 sharp, so she was ready for any customer who had an early morning need to be taken care of. Several of the local farm owners had come in for supplies, or agricultural products, or feed for their livestock. About three hours after they had opened the store, two of the young men of the area stopped in to buy some cigarettes and beef jerky. They were surprised to see a young girl behind the counter instead of Bill, who had owned the store for thirty years. They exchanged glances as they realized that Holly was alone in the store.

"Well, now, looky here," exclaimed Danny Potter to his friend Johnny Wilson.

"Looks like we got ourselves a little jelly bean for a store proprietor. What do you know about runnin' a real business, lil' missy?"

Holly's green eyes blazed. She clenched her jaw, and a lock of her sandy golden hair fell forward over one eye.

"I know enough about it, and I'll thank you to mind your manners, you two ruffians. Mr. Talbot trained me real well, and he knows I can handle things."

"Oh, yeah?" said Danny, the taller one. "Well, we're just about the best customers this ole store will ever have, and we figger that we got a few packs of butts and some beef jerky comin' to us. Now is a good time to take them 'cause we're a little down on our luck, missy."

Holly thought to herself, "What is the best thing to do? We can't afford to lose any profit this month." She turned to look out the small window behind the cash register, a little out of sight for the young troublemakers.

"Well, look here, now. It's Constable Barlow comin' in for his late-mornin' cup of coffee. Would you like to join him, boys?"

At the thought of running into the local constable, who was one tough character, the boys quickly exited by the side entrance, dropping the cigarettes and beef jerky as they ran.

"Whew," said Holly to herself. "I guess I'd better be prepared for anything if I'm going to get anywhere in this world." Holly was a quick study, and had a lot of good, natural courage, gleaned from her demanding life on the small farm. The rest of the day was uneventful, but Holly was still a little nervous, thinking of how differently things could have gone.

People came in for staples and supplies that were commonly in stock, and Holly had no trouble filling their orders and making them feel perfectly at ease, even with Bill away. A few customers asked where he was, but most were so used to seeing Holly and enjoyed her easy friendliness, that they preferred to deal with her. Andy, now age fourteen, stopped by to see his sister, and being curious about the prospect of her running the store alone, was happy his dad had let him run to town for a couple of hours.

Andy was very big for his age, and looked at least seventeen. He was tall like his dad, but more solidly built. Hard work had made his muscles firm. He was very close to his older sister, and the two of them had a nice visit, as Holly brought out a freshly baked coffeecake. She cut off two slices and enjoyed a few minutes of uninterrupted pleasure, chatting about business and life away from the farm.

Just as they were finishing up the last crumbs of their snack, Donny Walton came in, excited with worry and talking much too fast.

"Please help me, Holly, I just know you'll know what to do! Caroline is over at her ma's for the day, and the baby is hot with fever and tremblin' like I never see'd afore."

He held up the little boy, about eight months old, to show her his face, beaded with perspiration. He shivered every few seconds or so and was whimpering with discomfort.

"Poor baby," cried Holly. "Let me get a cool cloth to start with."

Holly ran to the back room and got a small towel, soaked it in cold water and laid it on his forehead. Then she filled a small washtub with cold water and immersed him in it. Immediately he started to relax, but still shivered. However, the rush of the fever went down and you could see that he felt more comfortable.

"I just got this medicine in from Columbia, a real good doctor recommended it for the fever. The two families that I have given it to said it was a lifesaver. You know the Clinton family over the ridge? They used it for their boy, Samuel, and he's doin' just fine now. Also, the Jacksons said it was fine for their grandma, who gets the flu easy like."

"Okay, then, go ahead." Donny felt that Holly knew what she was doing.

Holly gently gave the little boy a quarter tablet that she had crushed up and added some honey to for sweetness. Within ten minutes the baby relaxed and felt cooler to the touch, the shivering stopped. Holly dried him off and dressed him back in his clothes for his father.

"Now give him one quarter of a tablet in the mornin' and evenin' afore he goes to bed until the fever is gone. Maybe it'll take three or four days. Besides, Caroline will be home tonight, right, Donny?"

"Right," said Donny. "I can't tell you how much I 'preciate this, Holly. I was so scared, I felt like a possum with his leg caught in a hunter's trap! How can I repay you?"

"That smile on your face is all the thanks I need. You go home to your family, now and don't be thinkin' 'bout it again."

Andy watched as the relieved young dad went out and climbed into his pickup truck. He placed the baby on the seat next to him and drove off, waving his arm out the window as he headed for home.

"Boy, Holly. You sure knew what to do for that sick young-un. I was scared real bad. How did you keep so calm? I was real proud of you."

"Oh, Andy. It's just common sense, is all. Would you like to stay and help for a coupla' hours? I need a strong man to tote some of the sacks that people buy. They need help loadin' them in the trucks."

Holly thought her brother could use some appreciation for the work that he was always doing.

"Why, shore," exclaimed Andy. "I think Pa won't mind if I'm a little late comin' home. Paul and Henry are gettin' bigger and helpin' 'round the farm a lot more now, anyway."

The brother and sister enjoyed the time together for the rest of the afternoon. They worked well as a team and genuinely liked each other's company. Besides, Holly felt happy having someone else there after that morning's confrontation with the two ruffians. Andy was happy carrying the sacks of feed and flour the farmers bought, and had good conversations with them as they went through their lists of supplies.

At 7 p.m., Holly closed up and felt that all was secure and she was satisfied. Andy had left at five o'clock and wanted to get back home for his evening chores. Holly was concerned that she stay on top of everything in Bill's absence. She didn't want carelessness or busy activities to cause her to overlook something that could be critical to the welfare of the store. She was really beginning to become attached to it, and she enjoyed all aspects of running it. When the salesman came with his samples of yard goods every two months, she couldn't wait to see what was the newest thing from New York. Buying the large bolts of fabric was the fun part of stocking the store. Whatever she bought, all the ladies from the surrounding towns felt that she had a keen eye for choosing the best and bought lots of yard goods to make their families' clothes and household goods. Many of the ladies asked Holly's advice on how and what to make for their homes. Bill didn't like this part of the business, and he happily gave Holly free rein.

She locked up the store, hitched up the horse to the wagon and headed home in the cool, crisp, evening air of October. As she passed the fields near her home, she noticed the grass was turning its autumn shade of golden tan and the milkweed pods were a toasted brown color. The insides of the pods were white and shiny, wide open from letting the fluffy seeds fly in the wind. "Nature sure is beautiful," thought Holly.

As she went to bed that night she had visions of her own blossoming coming soon. She was eager to see just what was in store for her.

On Sunday morning, she awoke early, with anticipation of the last day on her own in the store. She hitched up the horse to the wagon and headed to town a full two hours before she had to open the store. Sunday shouldn't be too busy, she thought. Everyone would have gotten their orders on Saturday and then be in church for a good part of the day.

Things didn't go that way, though. This Sunday there was lots of activity. It was the third Sunday in October, and many of the farmers were harvesting their autumn vegetables—squash, turnips, pumpkins, and much of the staples they needed for the winter. They came in almost all day long to pick up various tools for harvesting and burlap bags to store vegetables down in the root cellars, built down in the ground under the houses to keep them cooler for the fall and protected for the winter. They came for the general supplies they knew Bill Talbot would have for them. Holly could have used Andy's help, but he was needed at home, and she managed fine without him. At five o'clock, Bill Talbot walked in the store with a smile of gratitude on his face and a hug for Holly for her good work.

"I knew I could count on you, Holly," he said. "How did it go?"

"Just fine, Mr. Talbot," replied Holly. "Nothin' to worry about. Business was good, and I felt real comfortable. How's your sister doin'?"

"She's better," replied Bill. "She sure was glad to see me. Get along home, now and relax. I'm sure you had a busy time alone."

"Okay, Mr. Talbot. I'll see you tomorrow at two o'clock." Her schedule at the store was two till closing, then all day Saturday.

The next day, Monday, when Holly came in at two o'clock Bill exclaimed to her, "Holly, I heard from Donny Walton this mornin', and he told me how you helped him with his sick baby and the fever. Jumpin' Jehosaphat, girl, you sure know how to handle a tough situation!"

"Oh well, Mr. Talbot, it wuzn't much. I've had a lot of experience with sick young-uns. It sure did take a load off his mind, though, with the missus away and all."

Bill Talbot never did hear about the two young roughnecks who gave Holly a hard time, but they never did come back in the store again, either. That made Holly happy.

That spring Elizabeth gave birth to her seventh child, another boy, named Clive. He was a big healthy baby and easy for Elizabeth to care for. He was six years younger than the closest girl, and that made a difference. Life was still a struggle on the farm, but things were a little easier because of the four younger ones being able to help in the fields and with the house chores. Anna was not much physical help, but she cooked for her mother and kept a cheery attitude.

Holly helped all she could, but her hours at the store took time from home. Elizabeth would have liked her help with the new baby, but Holly was seventeen now and wanted to make her way in the world away from home. She was determined not to be dissuaded. Elizabeth understood her daughter's feelings as she recalled her own dreams of a future as a young girl.

Billy Joe had begun to lose some of his health. The long days on the farm were taking their toll, and he had lost a lot of his enthusiasm after Selma had died. It was good that he could live here with Jed and Elizabeth and the family, but his own life had lost some of its individuality, and he blended in with the large brood even though he would have liked to be more independent. He helped a lot with the cotton crop, and the hard work around the farm itself, and Jed really valued having him there. Jed felt a lot of responsibility for his large family.

In the evenings, the two men would sit around the fireplace in the kitchen and rock, whittling small treasures for the children out of pieces of wood. Sometimes it would be a small doll or a whistle, or a little animal or comb for the girls' hair. Whatever it was, the children squealed with delight when it was finally finished and was presented to the one whose turn it was to get the toy.

The following year, when Clive was eighteen months old, Billy Joe passed away during the night. When Jed discovered that he was gone in the morning, he felt a sorrow that he never knew before. This was different from the pain he experienced when he lost his mother. He felt the loss of his best friend, which Billy Joe had become, because of all the tough times they had shared together over the years. Elizabeth, too, missed the man who had generously given so much to her and Jed, and made their life on the farm possible without ever expecting anything in return. "This is what being a parent is all about," she thought to herself.

Chapter 6
Striking Out in the World

Holly was offered a chance to go to New York City in the fall of her eighteenth year. This came about in a very unusual way, and Holly felt it was destiny. The salesman who came every eight weeks to take orders for fabrics was making a special trip to New York because a very large supplier of his had gone bankrupt. He had the chance to go and buy large quantities of goods at ninety percent off the normal price.

"Bill," he said. "I am taking my wife, Martha, with me to see the sights, and it would be perfectly all right to take Holly with the two of us. She could be a big help to me in choosing the best fabrics to buy at the discounted prices. Would she be able to come?"

Bill wasn't sure what to say, so he dropped by to talk to Jed and Elizabeth.

"I really feel that this is a good opportunity for Holly, Jed. She will be a big help. I know Martha and Jim Stanley very well, so she'll be in good hands. They'll drive up to New York on Monday, stay three days to buy, and be back by Tuesday of next week. Jim will pay for the hotel and expenses, and Holly will stay with Martha in her room."

When she heard, Holly was ecstatic. "Oh, Dad, please, *please*, I would die to see New York! Besides, think of all I'll learn!"

Holly had been polishing herself in many ways during these years in the store. She watched her vocabulary and practiced her diction so she could speak eloquently and with confidence. She was intent on being a successful and well-mannered woman.

"I don't know," started Jed. "The big city is a dangerous place. Any kind of terrible thing could happen. What do you say Elizabeth?"

Elizabeth looked into the green eyes that clung to every word and felt a pang in her heart that she knew would come over and over again as each of her little family began to set out into the big world alone. "Surely this is what Ma felt when she read the note I left for her that day nineteen years ago," thought Elizabeth.

"Jed, I think Holly is beginning to come into her own, and we can't deny her this chance."

"Okay," Jed replied, "If you really feel it's right."

Holly went to bed that night with the lightness of a milkweed seed sailing along on the evening breeze. She could hardly sleep at all.

Jim and Martha picked her up Monday morning early, just after sun-up. They drove off in Jim's pickup truck and headed southeast on Route 26, followed it to Columbia, then turned onto Route 20, heading north, and then east until it joined Route 95. The scenery along the way was fascinating for Holly. They passed through the beautiful wooded foothills of Sumter National Forest and then by the lakes that surrounded Columbia. It was all very green and lush. Holly loved the easy, relaxing pace of the South.

As they headed into North Carolina, the land became less hilly and there were fewer lakes. They made it all the way to Rocky Mount to spend their first night. Martha was a friendly woman and enjoyed the company of such a bright and well-mannered young girl.

"Tell me, Holly," she said. "Do you plan to be a businesswoman when you are older?"

"I am a businesswoman right now, ma'am. I am a beginner, though, and I need some more experiences to help me."

Martha admired her spirit, and resolved to give Holly the respect that she obviously wanted. "Well, we'll have a good time in New York, for sure, and you'll learn a lot there," she reaffirmed.

As they approached Washington, D.C., Jim turned from Route 95 onto Route 395. As they passed Arlington, Virginia, and the Arlington National Cemetery, they got a view, if distant, of the Washington Monument. Holly was speechless as she looked at the monument that stood taller than anything she had ever seen in her life.

"How could they build anything so tall?" she wondered. "I guess you can do anything if you put your mind to it." In her heart

Holly knew this to be the truth from the time she was a very young girl.

The area now was getting more populous, and Holly grew excited to see the change from the Virginia countryside and observe the constant goings-on of a large metropolitan area.

"People are dressed so nice," she exclaimed. "They must have important things to do, and this is what I want to be a part of."

Then they drove onto the Anacostia Freeway, circling the city and spent the second night outside of College Park, where they joined back up with Route 95 again. The little motel in College Park was clean and tidy, but it did smell a bit musty. They ate a hearty meal at the diner across the street to satisfy themselves and headed for bed, exhausted from the long day.

Holly could see that it was more built up and there were fewer green trees as they got closer to Maryland and Delaware. Next they drove onto the New Jersey Turnpike, and that took them straight to New York.

The traffic moved quickly, and Holly felt nervous, but she knew Jim was an experienced driver, covering the large area that he did in business. Martha was happy to be along, too. It wasn't very often that Jim offered to take her, but he knew how much she liked New York, and he felt she had been so understanding about his travel.

Martha had plans to buy three new dresses and maybe a hat in New York. She knew all her friends would be envious of her new purchases. They would never see such fine goods in Prairie Ridge for sure.

They exited from the turnpike and took the Staten Island Freeway across Staten Island, crossed the Verrazano Bridge, and drove into Brooklyn. Seventy-ninth Avenue was the address of the distribution center. The entire inside of the building, which was four stories tall, had been opened up to display hundreds of bolts of fabric of every type imaginable. The owner of the New England mill and many of his last remaining employees were stationed around in different locations to help sell off the goods.

There were beautiful heavy bouclés, damasks, chenilles, velvets, and anything you could imagine for bedspreads, upholstery covers, draperies, and tablecloths. The cloth for dresses and household goods was in another area. Holly was in paradise at seeing the wealth of fabric in front of her. She and Jim commiserated about what they needed and how much, so they wouldn't waste valuable time or miss out on anything by hesitating.

There were many buyers and owners of businesses there to take advantage of the marvelous prices and great selection. Jim needed his truck to be able to store the twenty-five bolts they decided on. Jim was calculating his profits already because of the large margin he would have with the deeply discounted goods. Holly picked out several bolts that she favored. She knew that the women of Prairie Ridge would snap the fabric up to make clothing for their families.

"Holly, you sure helped me make decisions here. It ain't easy, with all this to choose from, and you know the tastes of the local women."

Even Martha found herself asking Holly's advice when deciding between several different fabrics. They spent a day and a half buying goods and were quite satisfied about their purchases. Then they drove through the Brooklyn Tunnel to Manhattan so Martha could get her new dresses and hat. The shops were so elegant that Holly kept turning her head from one side of Fifth Avenue to the other. They drove down Park Avenue and then to the Avenue of the Americas. Martha chose one store that appealed to her, called Harbinger's, and they parked the truck on a lot and tipped the attendant to take care of it. The hard cover of the truck kept the goods out of sight. The three of them went inside and were speechless.

Harbinger's was a large department store and overwhelming in every way. The escalator, rows of glass and brass cases, the smartly dressed salespeople, everything that they saw was fascinating. They milled around for a while, but then found the dress department by the signs in the walkways. The pleasant saleswoman offered her services, and they told her what Martha wanted. She understood immediately, being experienced with all types of tourists and their tastes. She showed Martha some pretty, but practical dresses in her size, and Martha easily chose three.

When Martha mentioned a hat, the saleswoman chose the perfect complimentary hat for the dresses.

Within an hour and a half, they were finished and very happy with the choices. Holly was deeply impressed by all that she saw. She had felt a sense of fulfillment and capability in the general store that Mr. Talbot had shared with her for the past three years. But it was nothing like the sense of empowerment that surged through her now, while imagining what it would be like to run this kind of establishment.

As she stood there in the main aisle of the first floor, Holly noticed a well-groomed gentleman in his mid-forties, dressed in a formal-looking black suit, white shirt, and dark tie. He was observing everything that went on, stopping to greet customers and salespeople alike, as he meandered through the bright aisles. She knew that he must be the general manager by his air of authority. He wore a small brass nameplate stating simply, Mr. John Morgan. As he walked toward them, Holly seized the opportunity to speak graciously to him and wish him good day, complimenting him on the store.

"It is such a pleasure to be here and enjoy this lovely store, sir. You seem to have anticipated every wish and need a customer could imagine. We are so impressed with every aspect of it." Holly's eyes were alive with enthusiasm.

"Why thank you, young lady," replied the courteous gentleman. "It is our desire to have each and every customer come away with just that impression of Harbinger's."

He was impressed with Holly's beautiful appearance, but more so, by her eloquence, especially coming from one so young. He secretly wished that he might be able to add her to his staff. "Good day, now." He bade them farewell.

As they exited from the store and crossed the street to the parking lot, they felt a great satisfaction of a mission gone just as planned. They paid the parking attendant, having tipped him before to keep an eye on the truck. As Jim turned the key in the ignition, not a sound came out except for a dull click, the one that strikes fear in the heart of a driver with places to go and things to do.

"Oh, no!" they all exclaimed at the same time. "What has happened?"

"It is as dead as a doornail. What'll we do?"

"Don't worry," cried Holly. "I know what to do."

She jumped out of the truck, ran back across the street, and entered Harbinger's. Seeing Mr. Morgan walking down the aisle toward the back area of the first level, she quickly caught up with him.

"Oh, Mr. Morgan, sir. The worst thing has happened! Our ignition has gone dead. We need to call a service company to come and fix it. Do you know the name of a good mechanic? We have no idea who we can trust."

John Morgan felt a compassionate feeling for the gracious young girl and wanted to help if he could. "Here, come to my office and we'll make a call. I'm sure I know someone," he replied.

He took out the phone book and ran his finger along the row of numbers.

"Here it is." He dialed the number and spoke quickly. "Hello, Tim. You must come over to the store right away. We have an emergency. Yes, we have a dead battery. Fine." He hung up. "He'll be right over."

Holly relaxed immediately. She felt secure with Mr. Morgan taking charge of the dilemma.

"Tell me, young lady," he said. "How is it that someone as young as you is already worrying about her future and career?"

"I feel it is so important," her eyes sparkled. "Besides, I have a burning desire to go out in the world and make something of myself. I don't want to just stay in Prairie Ridge, South Carolina, for the rest of my life."

He sensed the determination that Holly kept inside, and he admired her spirit. He had hired many young people in his career in retail management, and he had a keen eye for spotting real talent. Holly rose from her chair and started for the door.

"I have to tell Jim and Martha that help is on the way. They'll be worried."

"Please have them come back here to my office while they wait for Tim to see what's wrong."

He had no intention of letting Holly slip away that easily.

"Why, thank you, Mr. Morgan. It shouldn't take a minute."

Holly ran across the street to inform Jim and Martha that help was on the way, just as Tim was pulling his tow truck into the parking lot.

"Things should be fine in a few minutes," said Holly. "This is a friend of Mr. Morgan's. He'll take care of us, I'm sure."

Tim pulled the truck next to Jim's and tried the ignition. It was unresponsive. Then he attached the cable clamps to Jim's battery on one end and the other clamps to his large battery under the hood at the other end. After two minutes, Tim tried the battery again. It was still dead.

"Well, it looks like there is another problem," Tim reported. "Let me see what I can find."

After a few minutes, Tim came around to speak to Jim.

"You need a new alternator here. It shouldn't take but half an hour to install it, but I show that I have none in stock. We'll have to wait two days to get one from the supplier."

"Well, order it then," Jim sighed. "I guess I have no choice."

"Let's go and see Mr. Morgan. He'll tell us where to get lodging for the night."

They locked up the truck and headed back across the street and into the store again. John Morgan was pleased to see the trio, but he sensed the defeat on their faces. "What is wrong?"

"Well, we have to stay two days for a part to come in. And we would like a recommendation of a good place to stay that is not too expensive."

Jim was reluctant to ask favors of a stranger. "We'll find a place, Mr. Morgan. Don't give it another thought. You are a busy man with a lot to do."

"Nonsense. There is a great place two blocks from here, and many of the vendors who visit me stay there. I'll reserve you two rooms right away."

"That sounds good." replied Jim. "We owe you one, for sure."

Mr. Morgan hung up the phone. "All set. Now why don't we all have some dinner in the restaurant on the sixth floor? I think I need some company tonight. I eat alone so often. It'll be a real treat for me."

It was difficult to refuse his generous hospitality, so they all headed for the sixth floor and some time to relax from the ordeal. They entered the lovely restaurant and noticed that it was quite busy, with a staff of attentive and pleasant servers. The decor of the restaurant was light and airy, with a magnificent view of the skyscrapers and just a corner of Central Park peeking through. Holly and Martha were feeling very special and felt that this was an extra treat for their trip, in spite of the inconvenience of the breakdown. Jim wished all of it had never happened and was trying very hard to keep a positive outlook.

Mr. Morgan led the way to the best table in the room, and they all sat down with two waiters escorting them.

"Please, let me order for all of us. I know what they do best, and I promise I won't pick anything that you will dislike."

"Fine," they all said and relaxed.

John picked an extra-large order of escargots for appetizers, and then came the soup of the day, which was cream of leek. All of them devoured both dishes in a short time, feeling that they had never enjoyed such scrumptious beginnings. After they had talked and relaxed a bit, out came filet mignon with potatoes gratinée for Jim, veal Parmesan for Martha, and rack of lamb for Holly. John had prime rib, which was his favorite. They all complimented their own dinners several times and told John how grateful they were for his generosity. They enjoyed the conversations and began to realize that it was time to plan for the night. John spoke up then.

"Holly, I was thinking," he began. "Since you have two days here and time will be heavy on your hands, perhaps you would like to have a little firsthand experience in the retail world of a New York department store."

"Well, Mr. Morgan. I certainly would love to see what it is really like here on a daily basis, but—"

"But nothing! There is a new girl who just started four weeks ago, and you could spend the night with her and work with her tomorrow to get a little experience. She is really nice. Her name is Peggy Newcomb. Jim and Martha, you both could stay just down the hall from the girls in the corporate apartment that we keep for out-of-town executives. I'll cancel your other reservations."

"Oh, I don't know." Jim hesitated. "I am responsible for Holly, and I would worry about her safety."

"Nonsense. She couldn't be safer. It's all decided, then! You'll stay."

Jim and Martha secretly felt that this might be a chance for them to see a little more of the city and Holly would be fine at Harbinger's, working all day. After all, what could they do? The truck was tied up for two days anyway.

"This sounds fine, Mr. Morgan. But could I meet Peggy first?"

"Certainly." Morgan was beginning to feel that things were looking up.

They took a cab three blocks south, nearer to Greenwich Village and got out in front of a moderately sized brownstone apartment building. The doorman greeted Mr. Morgan by name as they entered. They took the elevator up to the fifth floor and knocked on the door of apartment #508.

"I called Peggy before we left the restaurant. She is looking forward to meeting you all."

The door was opened by an attractive brown-haired girl, about twenty-two years of age. She was dressed in a crisp white blouse, dark skirt, and string of pearls around her neck.

"Hello, please come in and be comfortable," she said.

John spoke first. "Peggy Newcomb, this is Holly Cummings, and this is Martha and Jim Stanley. They are here from South Carolina on a buying trip, and Holly will be staying with you as we discussed."

"I'm delighted." Peggy's smile creased her round face. "We can have a lot of fun together, and I'll show you the ropes at Harbinger's, too."

They all sat around and had coffee and talked for about an hour, and then John said, "Let's go down the hall and I'll show you both your apartment, Jim and Martha." The apartment that they were to have was quite comfortable, and John made them feel right at home.

"Holly will come to work with Peggy in the morning, and I will give her a paycheck for the two days that she works, plus she'll get valuable experience in business to take back with her."

"That sounds good. She can use the extra money I'm sure, but what do you get out of it, Mr. Morgan?"

John Morgan hesitated. "I can really use a professional girl like Holly who seems to have such a good head for business, even if it is just for two days. I am short staffed. I think that her good example will rub off on the others." He was telling the truth. However, he had much more in mind than just two days.

Holly rose early Tuesday morning and showered and dressed before Peggy was up. They had talked late the night before, and Peggy slept in. Holly liked Peggy's easy ways, and they had a lot in common in spite of their three-year age difference.

Peggy had grown up in the Bronx and after high school had taken a job in a smaller retail shop. After three years' experience, she had applied to Harbinger's and been hired by John Morgan because of her polished ways and ability to get along with people. John put Peggy in the Better Dresses department, where she could make the best commissions. It had only been four weeks, but Peggy was making good sales, and everyone liked her, so John was happy. He only wished he had more like her. When he met Holly, he was elated because he felt she had the potential that Peggy had, only many times over. He had plans for Holly, and he wasn't going to let anything change them.

Holly and Peggy arrived at the store forty-five minutes early so that they could go over the stock, see what they had and in what sizes and make sure they and the store looked their absolute best.

When the store opened, customers came into Better Dresses and patiently waited to be taken care of by the capable young women. The first three or four ladies that Holly waited on were fairly easy to satisfy. However, a woman came in and started explaining to Holly just what she was looking for. Holly felt she understood what she wanted, even though she felt it was completely wrong for the woman. Her experience with fabrics and with the women of the general store had taught her what flatters certain types of figures and what brings out the worst attributes.

When she gently tried to get her point across, the woman screamed, "What do you think you know, anyway, you're just an ignorant salesgirl?"

Holly remained calm. She was not going to let an upset woman get to her.

"I was just trying to tell you that you have an extraordinary stature and that a vividly colored print does not do justice to the presence that you have as you enter a room in a social gathering," explained Holly in her best, patient tone.

The woman stopped, took a breath, and thought about what Holly had said.

"Do you mean that, or are you just trying to flatter me?" Her eyes evaluated Holly to get an honest answer.

"Certainly not," replied Holly. "This is my profession, and I care about what you choose and how you look when you buy a dress here at Harbinger's. Now if you look here in the full mirror, you can see how elegant this dress is when you wear it. Each dress looks differently on each woman, and each woman's shape dictates which type of dress consistently looks best. You can wear other types of dresses, but this type will always look wonderful on you."

The woman had to admit that what Holly said made sense. One look in the full mirror verified what she was saying.

"I'm sorry, dear," she said. "You are absolutely right. I was visualizing a look, but the reality is that this is the dress for me. You have made it a sure thing that when I go to my important party I will look smashing!"

"I'm glad I could be of help," replied Holly.

When she had taken her nicely wrapped parcel and departed, Peggy said, "Wow, Holly, I can't believe how you handled that woman! I have sold to her before, and she is very difficult."

"Well, I just put myself in the place of the customer and try to see things her way. That usually helps. Besides, service is the most important product that we have, right?"

As the woman was leaving the store, she stopped by the management offices and asked to see Mr. Morgan. She was aware of who he was and felt that she needed to talk with him.

"Mr. Morgan. You have yourself a gem out there in the Better Dresses department. Her name is Holly, and I was so impressed with her professionalism and genuine caring for me that I just had to stop by and let you know."

"Well, now, thank you, Mrs. Walters. I really appreciate hearing from you. You know I like to know everything that goes on, and incidentally, I agree with you whole-heartedly."

Mr. Morgan received another compliment about Holly that same day, and he observed her impressive behavior himself as he was making his rounds.

"I must keep her," he thought. "I would be a fool to let her get away. I have to figure out what it would take to get her to stay."

Meanwhile, Jim and Martha were enjoying the city. They went to the Empire State Building and Radio City Plaza to watch the goings on.

"I have to call Bill Talbot and tell him about the breakdown of the truck and be sure he lets Holly's parents know we'll be two days late getting back," Jim said uncomfortably.

When he called Bill, Jim explained the circumstances and assured him that Holly was safe and in good hands. He relayed the whole story of Harbinger's and John Morgan, which was impressive to Bill. When Bill, in turn, stopped by to tell Jed and Elizabeth Cummings the news, Jed reacted like any father of a young daughter would.

"I don't like this, at all! New York is too big a place, and too much could happen there. I want her home just as soon as that truck gets fixed up, no waitin' 'round, ya hear?"

Elizabeth had a hollow feeling in her stomach and she didn't want to explain it. The situation was too familiar to her.

Chapter 7
Career Opportunity

John Morgan called Holly into his office in the afternoon of her second day at Harbinger's. He had gone over in his mind and rehearsed in front of the mirror countless times what he would say to the bright young girl. He knew he only had a limited time to make his case, and he knew he had to make every word count. He hoped she was as mature as she seemed.

"Good afternoon, Holly. How is your second day going?"

"Oh, Mr. Morgan, it is fabulous! I love being involved in the business, and Peggy has been so kind to me. We are becoming good friends."

"That is what I like to hear, Holly. How would you like to remain close friends with Peggy and begin a permanent career here at Harbinger's? I would offer you a position of department manager for Better Dresses, and you could start with a very generous salary, indeed."

Mr. Morgan didn't let a word get in edgewise while he was making his offer. He wanted to give all the possible advantages before she thought of any negatives.

"Peggy is in the management program, and you could move in with her permanently and perhaps attend a couple of seminars, although you are already qualified to be department manager right now. The apartment she is in now is for people in training, and you wouldn't have to worry about rent for a while. I think she would be happy to have you, and you could be a big help to her in her career." John appealed to Holly's innate talent for helping others. Holly thought for a couple of minutes.

"Well, Mr. Morgan," she said. "You certainly caught me off guard with that offer, indeed! But what you say is true. I am eager to begin my career in business, and this is a special opportunity. Peggy and I get along really well, and having an apartment rent-free would be nice. How long would that be in effect, can I ask?"

"I would make it last for nine to twelve months, until Peggy has completed her management training program. Then you should have some money saved up and be able to find an apartment nearby in the right price range. Don't forget, your salary will increase as your sales increase, as you'll get commissions, too. I take care of my managers."

Holly hesitated again, thinking of her parents and young brothers and sisters. She would certainly miss them terribly, but the desire was so strong in her to build a career in business, that she could only concentrate on that. Certainly this type of opportunity would probably never come to her again, and it was a very unique set of circumstances that brought it to her. She was not going to turn her back on it, even though she felt she was letting Mr. Talbot down, too. Perhaps Mr. Talbot could use Anna to help out in the store a few hours a day. That would be good for her sister, too.

"Mr. Morgan, I really appreciate your offer. Could I have a few minutes to talk to Peggy about it also?" asked Holly.

"Of course you can. I'll get her from the floor, and she can talk with you here in my office. You can have your privacy."

Peggy came in a few minutes later and sat down, puzzled.

Holly began, "Peggy, I have had an offer from Mr. Morgan, and I am considering it. It would involve sharing your apartment with you for as long as you are in the management training program, and then finding a place of my own. Mr. Morgan has offered me the position of department manager of Better Dresses, which would mean that you would be working for me. Would that make you uncomfortable in any way?"

Peggy felt many conflicting thoughts run through her head, but she hid them all and showed only a happy smile and relaxed attitude. "No, of course not. We have become friends over the last two days and I would enjoy working with you a lot." Peggy realized how much Mr. Morgan thought of Holly, and she knew it would be suicide to fight against this. After all, she really did like Holly, and she did have her own career to think about, so she continued to smile. "I think it is a great opportunity for you. Congratulations!"

"Okay, then, I'll call Mr. Morgan in and tell him that I accept," said Holly. "I can't think of better news, you and me working and living together, wow!"

Mr. Morgan came into the office and thanked Peggy for coming by. He didn't know what to expect, but he had another ace in his pocket in case of a problem.

"Holly, I was thinking, probably you might like to go home and visit the family after Christmas, and that could be arranged. After the Christmas rush, you could take five days and go home to see everyone. That would give you two months to get acclimated here." He figured that offer would take away homesickness initially.

"All right, Mr. Morgan, you have a deal." Holly's face was bright with anticipation as she shook his hand to bind the agreement.

John Morgan felt a rush of excitement as he realized that he had accomplished what he set out to do two days ago, which at that time seemed such a long shot. Now Holly just had to break the news to Jim and Martha.

Holly went back to the Better Dresses department and continued working for the rest of the afternoon, making two more customers very happy and creating very large sales in the process. Peggy wondered why Mr. Morgan hadn't kept her in mind for the promotion of department manager. After all, she was older than Holly, with three years experience in an exclusive dress shop over on Second Avenue. She did admit to herself that Holly was very bright and had a special way with people, but Peggy couldn't get over the age difference. She thought of it much like rank in the military service.

Jim and Martha were happy to see Mr. Morgan and Holly waiting for them as they came into the store at 5:30, having gotten the truck back and being ready to begin the trip back to Prairie Ridge.

"Hello, you two," called John as they came toward them. "We have some exciting news to share. Holly has accepted my offer of an excellent position here at Harbinger's, and the start of an exciting and lucrative career for her!"

"What?" cried Jim. "Holly, you can't mean this! You are too young! What can I tell Bill Talbot and your parents? This is crazy!"

"Try to understand what a great opportunity this is for me," Holly exclaimed. "I will never get another one like this. The time is right for me. I have been planning my career for a long time and I am going to take this offer. Please explain to Mr. Talbot, and he'll tell my parents. I'll be home after Christmas, after the holiday rush. I am sure about this, and I won't change my mind."

Jim and Martha left the store feeling dejected, that they let their friends in Prairie Ridge down. After all, they had entrusted Holly's welfare to him, and now she was gone. How could he ever explain this? The trip home for Jim and Martha was joyless, thinking about Holly's decision to stay in New York and begin her future away from all those who loved her. The ride seemed to go by quickly, simply because they didn't want to have to face everyone in Prairie Ridge.

When they told Bill Talbot, he was shocked; it was something that he never expected. But he was quite impressed with the money and position that Holly had been offered. So when he went to give the bad news to Jed and Elizabeth, he stressed how important the position she had been offered was, and lucrative it would be. Elizabeth seemed to know that it was coming and didn't seem to be as shocked at the news.

The fact that Holly would come home in January helped soften the blow. Jed followed his wife's lead and was rather quiet about it. After Bill had left that evening, Elizabeth strolled along the dirt road by the house. She saw the dry milkweed pods still on the stems, but completely empty—all the seeds on fluffy parachutes had gone in the wind to settle elsewhere. "At least," she thought, "Holly will be home after Christmas."

Holly sat down at her desk to put together a letter to her parents, explaining in her own words how she had come to make this decision that would change her life so drastically. She explained how much she wanted to make her own place in the world. She knew that her mom understood, having struck out on her own at a young age. "I have a talent for business, and I enjoy using it and rising to meet the challenges it presents," she wrote. "I know you all will miss me, and I will miss you terribly, but the younger ones will help, and I will visit as much as possible." Holly closed the letter with a request: "Please wish me well, because I need it, and take care of the young ones for me. I love you, Holly."

Anna missed her twin a great deal but was the recipient of an offer to work part-time at the general store. She couldn't put in as many hours as Holly because of her less robust state of health, but she was also talented. She had a kind way with the customers, was just as accurate with the invoices, and enjoyed her time away from the farm.

Anna was a little smaller than Holly, with her mother's bright blue eyes and soft brown hair. They were fraternal, rather than identical twins, but happened to be the same gender. That was a plus for them, because people never confused them, and they always felt like individuals. Anna had observed Holly's successes at the general store and used all that she had observed to her own advantage. She did not have the innate perfect taste or the drive that Holly did, but she was bright and hard working. Bill Talbot was happy with Anna.

Things progressed well in Prairie Ridge through the fall, and into the Christmas season. Folks felt a festive air and were busy preserving, canning, and making homemade crafts for Christmas gifts.

In New York, Holly continued with her enthusiasm for Harbinger's and the retail management world that she had entered. She attended two seminars on business profits and projections, and buying and marketing. These were areas where she needed experience and more education, having had very little in the general store. After the seminars, she changed the buying decisions slightly, which seemed to work well. The new goods were well accepted and sold very well, making more profit. Her management skills were innately good, and she handled herself well with her subordinates. Peggy couldn't really point to anything that she objected to in Holly's management style, and they remained good friends.

Or so it appeared. Holly was comfortable and happy. She tried to do her best by Peggy, but she treated the other three girls in the department equally well, so there was no favoritism. Barbara was an older woman with good experience, but she had no drive to reach a higher position and liked Holly very much. Susan, who was in her mid-twenties, did not have the excellent sales skills to rise to the top, but she was a good worker and well liked. Nancy was an ambitious girl, about twenty-three, but she had a hard edge to her personality and John Morgan felt that charm was definitely a very strong point in his up-and-coming managers. During the two months that Holly had been at Harbinger's, she had record sales and countless customer recommendations that were given to Mr. Morgan and mailed in writing as well.

The Better Dresses department was enjoying an unprecedented profit margin and women, after hearing from their friends how talented and helpful Holly was, were flocking to buy everything for their wardrobes that was possible. Mr. Morgan couldn't have been happier, and during the annual December General Manager's Seminar held in New Orleans, he was presented the Recognition of Achievement Award for having the store with the most profitable department for 1979. This was quite an honor because there were sixty-seven stores in the chain, and all departments of all stores were included in the competition.

Naturally, he told Holly all about it when he returned and offered her a stock option of Harbinger's stock instead of a raise. Holly accepted happily, as she was not a person to live above her means and kept close tabs on her paycheck. She figured that some day, perhaps many years in the future, she could retire and cash in these few stocks.

The time had gone by so fast that Holly realized that the Christmas season was already here. The rush of business was gratifying, and she picked out a few gifts for her family as she tried to plan her trip home. It seemed to sneak up on her, and she knew that she could only go for a few days. On January 3, she hopped on a train that took her to Columbia in twelve hours. Andy was at the train station to pick her up in the horse buggy as she stepped from the train with her packages. She was so glad to see him that tears welled up in her eyes, and she couldn't wipe them away because her arms were full.

"Holly," he yelled. "Git in here fast, I cain't wait to see ya!"

Holly dropped the parcels and gave Andy a big hug, knocking him a little off balance. "You grew up!" she exclaimed. "You must be six feet now."

Andy was always happy around his older sister and felt that familiar glow again. "Wait'll you see what Ma made for ya . . . sweet potato pie, collard greens, black-eyed peas, roast goose . . . all your favorites," he said.

When they walked through the door, Elizabeth rushed up to hug her daughter, eyes full of tears, but a feeling of elation in her heart. "We've missed ya so much, Holly," she cried. "Things just ain't the same, no mo'".

"But, Ma, you know how I always wanted to be a business-woman. Now I am," Holly replied.

The younger ones all gathered around Holly, some up to her shoulders, some tugging on the hem of her skirt.

"I have gifts for everyone," Holly exclaimed. "Here, open them up now!"

Jed came into the front room and hugged his daughter with a bear hug that practically took her breath away.

"Pa," said Holly. "You forget I'm a girl!"

"No, siree," replied Jed. "That's for almost three months' worth."

"Did you get the checks I sent to help with the fall supplies?" asked Holly.

"Shore did, and thanks so much. You shore you could spare it?" asked Jed.

"It doesn't take much to take care of me in New York, you know. I share an apartment with a real nice girl and we split everything," she replied.

Anna was next and she hugged her twin for a long time, realizing just how much she had missed her.

"Anna, I have something extra-special for you." She had a large box, which was beautifully wrapped. As Anna opened the box, she realized inside was a beautiful wool winter coat. It was a deep wine color and had fur trim on the collar and cuffs.

"Wow!" cried Anna. "I cain't believe it! It's gorgeous. I can wear it to work at the general store."

"You bet," said Holly. "Don't save it for later. Wear it *now*."

After they had enjoyed a full meal with all the trimmings, they all sat around and exchanged stories.

"Tell us 'bout New York, Holly," cried several of the young ones. "What does it look like?" "Are the buildin's really as tall as the sky?"

"Almost," replied Holly. "They are all so close together that sometimes you can't even see the sky. Do you believe that? There are many, many people on the street all the time, and they never say 'hello' or 'how are you?'. It's a very different place from Prairie Ridge, but it is very exciting."

Holly felt strangely out of place as she went to bed that night with Anna and one of the older girls in one of the three small bedrooms. She had forgotten how crowded it was in the small house. "It's strange how quickly one adapts to change," thought Holly, "especially when it's something you love."

The family visit went by quickly. The entire family just hung on Holly's every word, and had many questions to ask, but she never ran out of patience. She realized how small their world was, and how she had brought just a tiny slice of the outside world to them, and they cherished it. On the afternoon of the fourth day, Andy pulled Holly aside and asked, "Do ya think there might be somethin' for me in New York? I would love to be able to go and see how I like the big city, Holly."

Holly felt his anxiety, and replied, "Andy, you are only seventeen, there is a lot of time for you still. Let's plan for something in the next two years to see how you feel then, and what opportunities I can line up for you."

"Okay, sis," he replied, knowing that his sister would keep her word.

That night, knowing she had to get back on the train in the morning, Holly felt sad. It would be a while before she could come home again. Just as she was climbing into bed, Elizabeth came into the room and stole a moment with her alone, before the other girls came to bed, too.

"Holly, y'all know how much I miss ya and wish ya could stay here always. But, I had dreams, too, when I was young. If you don't go after them now, ya never will have 'nother chance. Jus' be shore that they're what you want."

"Ma," replied Holly. "I really appreciate your being so understanding. I know it's hard here on the farm and all, but the younger ones are helping a lot, I see. I promise I'll write and send a check whenever I can. Of course, I'll come home again as soon as I can. I really do love what I'm doing in New York."

The next morning Holly boarded the train in Columbia for New York City. It was two years before she could get back to the little farm again.

When Holly arrived back at Harbinger's, John Morgan called her into his office first thing.

"Holly, there has been a small crisis when you were away. It seems that Mrs. Donald Parkerton's check for $2,000 never got deposited into the store account. I thought that you did that before you left for home."

"I did, Mr. Morgan. I specifically remember doing that the evening before I left. It was for the three new dresses she bought for her cruise. I put the check in with some others that were smaller and made the deposit."

"This is serious, Holly. We have to be able to rely on you to follow through with your responsibilities. I have to look into this. I have looked behind the cash register to see if it fell there and missed getting into the envelope for the bank. It was not there. I also asked Peggy, Barbara, Susan, and Nancy if they had seen it. No one saw it or knew anything about it. Peggy should have at least seen it, if she is training to be an assistant manager, however—"

Back on Monday, Holly had been preparing her department to run smoothly while she would be home visiting her family. She had been making up the deposit slip for the bank deposit at the end of the day. The phone rang, and it was for her, so she took the call on the phone at the other side of the department, enabling the other girls to use the front cash register and desk. This all started to come back to her as she thought it out. When she had finished speaking to Mrs. Willoughby about her upcoming cruise and potential purchases, she returned to the desk, opened the drawer, and put the paper-clipped pile of checks and deposit slip into the pouch to take to the bank's night deposit slot. Peggy had stepped back as she took the pouch and offered to walk with her, but Nancy interrupted. "I'm going that way to catch my bus. I'll walk with you, Holly."

"Hmm," thought Holly, "I wonder if Peggy noticed anything."

"No, I didn't see anything unusual, Holly. The checks were in the pouch, and all was normal," Peggy replied.

"Well," said Holly, "I am in big trouble, because Mr. Morgan thinks I am careless, and we are out the money. Oh, I know Mrs. Parkerton would write another check and put a stop payment on the first one, but it's just so awkward for me."

"Don't worry," said Peggy. "It'll all work out." She had a look of discomfort on her face that Holly had not seen before.

Peggy got off her shift at six o'clock that day and went directly to the apartment that the girls shared. Holly was scheduled until nine and remained in the store. Peggy went straight to her room and opened the top drawer in her dresser, and from underneath her pantyhose, she pulled out the $2,000 check written by Mrs. Parkerton. "It just isn't fair that Holly gets this position, and I am overlooked," she thought. "Holly needs to have a few things go wrong, so that Mr. Morgan won't think she is so great. Then I'll have a chance at a promotion. After all, I really deserve it. No one will ever know, because I'll put the check back behind the register as if it fell. If Mrs. Parkerton writes another check, then it is useless for me to keep this one."

The next day, Peggy had the late shift, and Holly was off at six. She went directly home to try to relax and figure out what might have happened to the check. It still puzzled her, as she knew she had deposited it. Ten minutes after closing, Mr. Morgan was doing a final walk through to make sure the store was secure for the night, when he saw Peggy at the register, and the lights were out, except for the small ones that provide dim light throughout the store. She didn't see him and was fussing around down on the floor behind the counter area. "What could she be doing at this hour in the dark?" thought John. He stepped behind a pillar and watched her go by as she left the store for the night.

"Good night, Ted," she said to the doorman as she left.

John walked over to the counter, and looked behind the register area with the flashlight that he borrowed from Ted. Behind the register was the Parkerton check, as big as life. He knew that he had looked before, and it was not there then! "So, we have a little skullduggery going on, do we?" said John to himself. "Well, we'll get to the bottom of this."

The next morning Peggy was in at nine, and John called her into his office right away. He had thought long and hard during the night about what to do. He knew that she and Holly were friends, yet this was a serious problem. John had dealt with this type of situation before, and he knew what the future held. Once an employee was dishonest, it was hard to trust him or her again. Peggy knocked on the door, and he asked her to come in.

"Good morning," she said, cheerily. "What's going on today?"

"Well, Peggy, I would like to clear up just a few more things about the missing check from Mrs. Parkerton, please come in and sit down."

Peggy's eyes clouded with confusion, and just a hint of fear that was hardly discernible.

John continued, "Early this morning the cleaning crew found the check behind the register in Better Dresses. I don't know why it sat there for so long."

"Well, Mr. Morgan, maybe it was so far back, that we just didn't look hard enough," explained Peggy.

"Peggy," he began. "I looked there myself, and believe me I looked very thoroughly. Besides, I saw you doing something behind there last night after closing. What is going on?"

Peggy hesitated. "Mr. Morgan, really, I don't know what you mean. I had nothing to do with that check's disappearance." Her eyes began to blink. "It isn't fair, I am a good employee . . . I . . . really—" she covered her face with her hands. "It isn't fair that Holly got the position of department manager when I should be the one. I am older and more experienced than she is. I have been here longer. She is just a new person and doesn't know Harbinger's like I do."

"Holly was given the position by me because of her experience as a store manager, which she has been for three years, and also because she has extraordinary sales talent and has made that department more profitable and run smoother than it ever has. She is a fair and capable manager and I thought everyone in Better Dresses was getting along well. Where did this come from? We don't have any place for a dishonest sales associate in Harbinger's, especially one that has every advantage and opportunity offered to her. You can pick up your things from the apartment and leave by the end of the day."

Mr. Morgan felt disappointment. He had plans for Peggy, feeling that she could, in time, follow in Holly's footsteps. He also hated to tell Holly how she had been betrayed by someone whom she felt was a friend. Peggy walked out of the office, never fully understanding what a miserable, unnecessary trick she did to further her own career at the expense of another's.

At noon, when Holly came in for her shift at the store, Mr. Morgan called her into his office and asked her to have a seat.

"Sure, Mr. Morgan," she replied, wondering what was going on.

"Holly, I have some troubling news," John began. "It seems we have located the Parkerton check. Apparently, Peggy took it from the deposit that you made the night before you left and kept it so that you would get into trouble and maybe lose your position. She felt that she should have had the position as manager and that you did not deserve it. I have gone over this with her and I saw her trying to put it back behind the register last night myself. There is no doubt about this, Holly. I have let her go, and we just have to keep moving forward."

"Oh, no, Mr. Morgan," Holly gasped. "I can't believe this about Peggy. I thought we were good friends. That she would never do anything to hurt me. Why would she do this?"

"She had her own plans for Better Dresses, and that included herself as manager." explained John. "Now go out there and show me what you are made of, and have the best day you ever had."

Holly set her jaw in the position that she did when adversity came her way and walked out of the office determined to make her day the best. She was very busy and her sales were unusually good. Holly was glad that she had a lot to do, because her heart was heavy with Peggy's betrayal. She explained to Susan, Barbara, and Nancy that Peggy had to leave because of personal reasons, and she left it at that. The girls knew that something was wrong, but didn't dare to pry further. They knew that Holly was a private person.

Peggy had left John Morgan's office frustrated and without any idea of what to do. She went over to the Hotel for Young Women on 46th Street and took a room. She waited until noon, when she knew Holly would have left for work and then went to the apartment and took all her belongings over to the new room.

"I'll get even with them if it's the last thing I do," thought Peggy. "They won't get away with it, they'll see."

When Holly came home from work at nine, the apartment was noticeably different. Peggy's things were gone, and the place looked pretty bare. The furniture belonged to the apartment, naturally, but both girls had added a few of their personal possessions, and that made it homelike. The pretty little wall hanging of dried flowers of Peggy's was gone. All the family photos and little bedside lamp, over which they had draped a scarf for atmosphere, were gone. Holly felt abandoned. She made herself a cup of tea and went to bed, trying to put the sad day behind her.

"I guess I have to get used to it, that people will let you down, and you can't let it get to you and spoil your life. I must learn from this, and go forward," she thought.

Mr. Morgan was relieved when all the facts of the unfortunate situation came to light. He hated to think that Holly, whom he had sensed had a great future with Harbinger's, would turn out to be so careless. Now, he felt things would progress as he had planned.

Chapter 8
A Change of Direction

Holly had an uneventful spring at Harbinger's. There were several young women who applied for the vacancy left by Peggy, and Holly interviewed them all and then sent her choice to see John Morgan. He agreed that the one Holly chose would be good. Her name was Sandra Lynch. She was twenty-five and had several years in retail selling. She was aggressive, but not too much so, and Holly felt comfortable with her. Susan became her right-hand person after Peggy's departure and helped with all the duties of the department.

Things were running smoothly, and Holly was content. In late May, Holly was sent a notice that she would be attending a manager's seminar in Los Angeles, networking with some of the better vendors that she dealt with. She hated to be away from the store, but she was eager to enjoy the beautiful weather of Los Angeles and see the city that she had heard so much about. The seminar was to last four days. They arrived in the late morning of the first day, and had a lunch meeting from one o'clock until five. This was an introduction meeting, and then four representatives were introduced.

The first was a man in his mid-forties, representing Pierre Designs, a top designer line. He was quite pleasant and made sure to spend time with each manager to see if they had any questions. He had been in the business for twenty-four years and knew all there was to know. The second man, named Jack Navarro, was in his late twenties, and was devastatingly handsome, with his thick sandy hair, bright deep-set blue eyes, and chiseled chin. He had become involved in the world of fashion on leaving NYU after his sophomore year. He had worked hard for a year, and then was offered a representative job for the Malaga Line, a designer line from Spain. Jack had become enormously successful at this, with his easy style and riveting good looks. He had superb taste and equally superb manners.

Milkweed

When Holly was introduced to Jack, he caught his breath for a second, and then a relaxed smile spread across his face.

"It is such a pleasure to meet you, Holly", he said. "I believe I have heard your name as the Manager of the Year. That's quite an honor so early in your career, but I can see why you were chosen, in addition to your sales record and management success, of course."

Holly thought that he was a little too sure of himself, but she couldn't help liking his easy, confident style.

"Well. You don't really know anything about me or my capabilities, don't you think that's a superficial opinion?"

Jack was caught off-guard. Usually when he turned on the charm, people, especially women, absorbed it, and did not criticize. "I'm sorry if I seem to give out false compliments," he said. "But I noticed your natural beauty and professional demeanor. That is what I meant."

"Okay, let's forget it," she replied. "We have too much to accomplish here to waste time on nit-picking."

The rest of the afternoon was spent on information and questions that the managers might have about the new lines. After they headed back to their own rooms at the hotel, the managers relaxed a bit and changed to go down to dinner. Harbinger's had arranged a lovely buffet dinner on one of the terraces of the hotel. It was especially lovely, because the hotel was on the water at Santa Monica. The steep cliffs, covered with fuchsia bougainvillea plants were on one side, and the wide, green Pacific on the other. Holly felt that she was in paradise.

There was heavy traffic on the busy Pacific Coast Highway, which ran below the hotel, but no one noticed it because of the idyllic setting. As she was standing at the buffet table, deciding what looked best, Jack came up to her, dressed in a light blue sport shirt with an open collar.

"Hi. What a wonderful buffet. I don't know what to take. Help me with my choices, please, Holly."

"Well," Holly hesitated. "I was just thinking the same thing."

"Do you like new and exotic foods, or do you stick to the familiar ones?" Jack asked.

"Well, I'll try new things," Holly said. "I'll take a chance."

"Why don't you go a take a seat, then, and I'll get plates for both of us and you can enjoy a surprise." Jack was his most charming self.

"Okay, then, surprise me."

Jack was elated. He knew he had made up for some of the bad impression that he had made earlier. He chose very carefully for Holly. First, he chose the fresh lobster, out of its shell, in seasoned butter sauce. Then he added fresh mixed cold green and yellow vegetables in dill dressing. An elegant potato salad made of small red potatoes was next, and then a hot roll with butter. He chose the same for himself. A server came around and gave them both tall frosty glasses of iced tea.

"Perfect," exclaimed Holly. "How did you know?"

"Just guessed, that's all," he replied.

They enjoyed their dinners together and talked about the business and family. Jack had only one sister, who was two years younger, and was fascinated that Holly had six brothers and sisters, let alone a twin.

"Do you miss them a lot?" he asked.

"Yes, of course, but in a big family, one has to assert his or her independence or you get lost in the shuffle."

They talked on and on, feeling more and more comfortable with each other as the evening progressed. When dessert was served, they took a break from talking and enjoyed the juicy red California strawberries heaped on angel food cake and covered with whipped cream. Holly couldn't remember a better day in her entire life.

Jack walked her back to her room by eleven, as the next day started early with a breakfast meeting. He looked deep into her eyes as he said good night, and he felt magnetized by the sparkling green eyes that were the color of the Pacific Ocean just outside. Holly would have liked it if he had kissed her, but she knew that was not right. He was a business affiliate, and things needed to be kept on a business level.

The next morning, when she entered the sunny, flower-bedecked salon where breakfast was being served, she did not see him. She felt a stab of disappointment but said to herself, "Don't be a fool, you probably will never see him again, and that's all for the good." The meeting got started and there was much discussion of profits, projections, and buying trends. Some of the managers made comments, and others discussed these points.

Holly got up and made a strong point for changing of some of the long-held buying traditions that had really gone out of style. Her point was well taken, and several managers and a regional director complimented her on her astuteness. When the meeting was half over, she saw Jack come in the side door, trying not to disturb the meeting. He sat down in the closest chair and looked her way. She smiled and then turned her attention to the speaker.

When there was a break for people to move around for a few minutes, he came over to her and said, "I had a small crisis from corporate, but it is taken care of now."

After the break, the chairman of the meeting announced that each of the representatives would have some time to talk about their lines and answer questions. The first two representatives talked on and on about their lines, giving some good information, but really just killing time, and then asked if anyone had questions. Several of the managers did have some questions and some discussion did ensue.

Jack was the third to speak. Holly felt that he was far superior to the other two. He had some beautiful illustrations with him and gave a good projection of the summer and fall line-ups that Malaga had in store. There were exciting designs and some really innovative ideas. Holly could not help but be impressed. Jack felt nervous during his presentation because he wanted to be so perfect in front of Holly. He had never met anyone like her before—beautiful, very bright, confident, capable, yet soft-spoken and kind. He felt a little off balance.

The fourth representative spoke, and then they all adjourned to their rooms to prepare for dinner. Holly was exhausted from all the activity and brainstorming, so she lay on her bed for a quick nap. She slept for an hour and a half and awoke with a start.

"Oh, no," she cried. "I have to be down for dinner in twenty minutes. I'll never make it!"

She quickly showered and threw on her sheer, pale green sundress. There was no time for make-up, so she just dabbed her lips with gloss and touched some mascara to her long lashes. After running a comb through her hair, she headed for the dining room. The majority of the managers were just coming through the door and she felt she squeezed in, just in the nick of time. Jack came over to her immediately, smiling and eager to see her.

"Oh, gosh," Holly stammered. "I fell asleep and just woke up. I was afraid I would be late. I just threw my dress on, and here I am."

"Pretty impressive," exclaimed Jack. "Most girls have to put make-up on in front of the mirror for forty-five minutes before they go anywhere." He admired Holly's clear skin and natural blush in her cheeks. Her green eyes were bright and rested. "We had better sit down," he continued. "The entertainment is about to begin."

The lights dimmed, and a magician with his attractive young assistant walked out onto the center of the stage. Holly had never seen a really professional magician perform before, and her eyes grew wide with astonishment as he pulled live birds out of his sleeve, made his assistant disappear from a locked wooden crate, and performed various tricks that delight tourists and regular magic show attendees alike. Jack liked watching Holly enjoy the show and marveled at her spontaneity and child-like wonder. "This girl is truly one of a kind," he thought, "and I do not intend to let it end here in Los Angeles."

During dinner Holly was relaxed and chatty. She knew that there was only one more day left to enjoy all this excitement, and she wanted to do it all. After a particularly delicious dinner of fresh grilled salmon and all the trimmings, they walked out along the edge of the winding path that ran along the ocean. It was soothing, yet exciting to hear the breaking of the waves on the steep cliffs. There was much erosion, so there were no rocks along the shore, the way it was on the East Coast by the Atlantic Ocean. "Such a sad thing to see," thought Holly. "In time, the shoreline will take away many of these beautiful homes and even the highway as well."

Jack thought she was the most beautiful girl he had ever seen in the moonlight there, along the Pacific, and he turned, pulling her up into his arms and gently kissed her on the lips.

"Oh," gasped Holly, "we shouldn't, we should have a professional relationship."

"I'm sorry," Jack apologized. "I just couldn't help myself. I have never known anyone like you before. Why can't we have both, a professional and a personal relationship? No one needs to know."

Holly thought a minute. "We'll see," she said quietly. She was so attracted to Jack; his easy charm, his striking good looks, and his sophistication were hard to resist. However, she had reservations about becoming involved with someone she would have business connections to.

"Let's call it a night," she said. "Tomorrow starts early."

Holding hands, Jack walked her to her room, and they said goodnight.

The next day they were to depart, but they had a short breakfast meeting that ended by ten o'clock. Jack was sitting with some of the other managers when Holly came down, and she was secretly relieved, as she wanted to be able to leave without any discomfort. She hated good-byes and thought, "good, I'm off the hook."

However, after the meeting concluded, Jack came over and said, "I will be coming to the New York store in July, and I'll look forward to seeing you."

"Great," replied Holly. "I'll see you then, and I hope you have good road trips until then."

She hoped that by July, her feelings for him would have dissipated. They shook hands good-bye, and her heart fluttered in her chest.

When Holly returned to Harbinger's, she reported what she had learned about the fall line-up to John Morgan and discussed at great length her opinions and perceptions about the buying practices for Malaga, Pierre, and Bocari and Turturro. Holly's input was very valuable, as she was incredibly perceptive and had opinions that were not hasty or emotional. They were trying to cut down the excess buying that Harbinger's had been guilty of lately. In her absence, Better Dresses had run smoothly and had showed good figures every day. Holly was relieved, as she worried what would happen while she was gone. Between Susan and Sandra, things ran well. Sandra was eager to assume responsibility, and Susan was always reliable.

Before she knew it, July had arrived. Jack called and informed her that his visit to her store was going to happen in the middle of the month. Holly felt uneasy because she knew she still had feelings that she had not dealt with about him. She felt uncomfortable about getting involved with him when he was someone that she would see regularly in business. She had not seen him before, because his visits were not on a regular schedule and the goods from Malaga arrived at certain intervals, with information pertinent to them on printed letterheads from the corporate offices in Madrid. Now, she knew that she would be seeing Jack on a regular basis and this she had misgivings about, even if he did not.

Jack arrived just as he had said, on July 15. He looked just as handsome as ever, and he had a big smile for Holly as he greeted the other girls in Better Dresses. They were hanging on his every word. Only one of them had met Jack before, and that was Barbara, who was not in his age category. Jack was very knowledgeable about fashion in general and his products specifically. He usually stayed in town for two days helping the salespersons with the customers and introducing the new styles from Malaga for the upcoming season.

His skills as a salesman were impressive. It seemed every woman followed what he said to a T. He instantly sized up each woman's figure flaws and personal taste. He communicated with them quickly. He made it seem so easy; Susan, Sandra, Barbara, and Nancy wished that they had his talent with the customers. Holly did, too, but she had her own skills and she knew it.

At the end of the first day, after all the other girls had left, Jack asked Holly, "Let's grab a bite to eat, you must be famished."

"Okay," she replied, "I *am* starved." As they crossed the street, he stopped at a flower vendor, and took two of his most beautiful bunches and gave them to Holly.

Over dinner at a small Italian restaurant near Harbinger's, he reached for her hand, "I have missed you, Holly. I couldn't wait to see you." He leaned over and kissed her gently, as they were sitting side by side. Holly felt herself give in. "He is so well mannered and thoughtful," she thought, "and these flowers he bought me are lovely." They enjoyed a delicious meal and chatted about Harbinger's and the fashion industry in general.

"You know, I really like the business," confided Jack. "It is challenging and creative for me, and I never get tired of making the rounds of all the stores. Each one is different and has its own culture. The big chains and the smaller ones, and the individual, exclusive boutiques, all present different challenges for me."

"I feel the same way, Jack," Holly said. "I love my job, too, and I know there is also a lot ahead for me in the future. At least, I hope so."

Then Jack looked into her eyes and said, "I have missed you these two months, Holly. I couldn't wait to come to see you. I am coming back here in August, and then let's plan for something special together."

Holly hesitated, "What do you mean by special, Jack?"

"Well, a play maybe, and I'd like to introduce you to some of my friends."

"I guess it couldn't hurt," Holly said. "It sounds like fun."

The next day Jack worked with the customers and the Malaga Line was selling like never before. Both of them were pleased. At five o'clock Jack said, "I have to go now, Holly. I have to be in Washington, D.C., in the morning for an opening at Southwick's Department Store, but I'll call you in a few days, and I'll see you in August."

He did call and filled her in about his activities and told her that the play they would see was the new Broadway sensation. Holly was thrilled, as she had heard raves about the play.

They went to a performance, and meeting some of Jack's friends was interesting. Most of them were professionals or in sales, and they were in their thirties. They were a friendly group and obviously enjoyed themselves, coming from privileged backgrounds. Holly wasn't used to this type of social lifestyle, and it seemed that they didn't take very much seriously.

On a Tuesday morning, not soon after, Holly was watching the morning news on TV, when she happened to notice a report on the stock market. It showed some stocks that had appreciated, and she noticed Harbinger's showing at $10 per share. "Boy," she thought, "I had better remember to exercise my option to buy those thousand shares of stock before I lose it. It was within three years, and it's close to that now. Also, it was at five dollars per share when I got it, so I have made double my money without doing a thing! This is great!"

She had put away $4,000 since working at Harbinger's, in addition to sending money home for the family. She figured that she could get a loan for the extra thousand from her bank, which was also the company bank, and they knew her well. "Thank goodness I have been able to talk to Mr. Morgan about these options, and make sure that I keep them," she thought.

For the next few months, Holly and Jack saw each other just about once every month, and he called her every two or three days on the phone. She felt extremely happy with her professional life and personal life going so well.

Chapter 9
Moving Up

John Morgan called Holly into his office on a cool morning in October. "Holly, I have some great news."

"What is it?" she asked.

"There is a vacancy as the western regional manager in Women's Better Dresses, Bridge Fashions, and Designer that came up, and I recommended you for that position. Corporate called me this morning and told me that you have it!"

"Oh, my Lord! I can't believe it! Thank you so much, Mr. Morgan. When do I start? Where do I go? Who will take over Better Dresses? Oh my gosh!"

"Take it easy, young lady. One thing at a time. You start next week. You will be here in New York, but you will travel some. Sandra will take over Better Dresses. She has been doing a good job assisting you, and I have confidence in her. I haven't told her yet. I wanted to get your reaction first."

Holly decided that she and John would break the news to the girls about Sandra's promotion together. They called a meeting at 5:30 that afternoon, just at the end of the early shift, which got off at six o'clock, so they could have all the girls there at the same time.

John Morgan broke the news, "I have some exciting news for you all, girls. There has been a change in positions that we all can celebrate. Holly has just been promoted to western regional manager in Women's Better Dresses, Bridge Fashions, and Designer. We all know that she has worked hard for quite some time, and we all feel she is well deserving of this honor. Now, Holly and I feel that Sandra should be appointed to the position of manager of Better Dresses."

Everyone gasped. They all were proud of Holly and knew that she would move ahead in Harbinger's, without any doubt. Susan and Barbara were happy for Sandra, and said so, with big smiles on their faces. However, Nancy was surprised and had secretly hoped that she would be the next one in Better Dresses to get a promotion. She hid her feelings with a smile and congratulated Sandra. No one noticed that there was a lack of sincerity in her voice.

There were a few more questions, for Holly about her schedule and duties, and the girls went back to work. Nancy was finished for the day at six o'clock and went out and down the aisle toward the large double front doors. She saw Mr. Morgan returning to his office just a few steps behind her, and stopped to speak to him.

"Mr. Morgan, could I have a few minutes of your time, please?"

"Why, of course, Nancy. Come in. What can I help you with?"

Nancy started, "I just wanted to talk to you about the position of manager of Better Dresses. Somehow I felt that I might have a shot at it, having been here longer than Sandra, and also, I really do have better sales figures than she does."

"Well, I am glad that you came to talk to me about this. I would like to go over some of the other qualifications that a person needs to have to become a department manager. It is true that you do have excellent sales figures. Also, you are a hard worker and very thorough.

"However, there is one area that you do need to work on, and that is your people skills. I really would like to see you have a little more understanding and patience with your co-workers. I am referring to the other day that you changed schedules with Barbara because of her doctor's appointment, and you grumbled about it and really made her feel guilty before you finally gave in and did it. Also, the times that you have debated with your customers about a markdown price or a return that you really didn't want to take. All these things leave a bad impression in people's minds. I would like to see you handle things with a little more graciousness. Harbinger's prides itself on service and encouraging the customer to return."

"Very well, Mr. Morgan, I will make an extra effort to polish my people skills. Sometimes, I have to stop and concentrate on it because things just come out quickly."

"Fine. I promise I'll notice if you try, and you will be the next person that I keep in mind for promotion. Thanks for stopping by. See you tomorrow."

"Good night, Mr. Morgan," said Nancy.

Holly moved to her new corporate office the next day. It was located over on Avenue of the Americas on the twentieth floor of an ultramodern office building. She had an office between the director of advertising, who was in the corner with a fabulous view, and the director of marketing. Her responsibilities were to coordinate all departments under her domain, and monitor the buying, promotions, and product mix. This was a big challenge because it gave her more control and creativity with the goods. "Boy," she exclaimed at the end of the first week. "I had no idea there was so much involved. I am inundated with vendors who want to supply goods to us."

Jack called her at her new office the second day and congratulated her heartily, saying, "They couldn't have made a better choice, darling. You were made for the job."

"Oh, Jack. Now you'll have to make an appointment to see me. You'll have to get by my secretary," she laughed.

"No problem, sweetheart. That's my specialty."

The months went by, and Holly's twenty-fifth birthday was around the corner. Jack wanted to go somewhere special to celebrate and have a big party with lots of people to make a fuss.

"Jack, I just want to have a nice dinner, maybe invite your friend Josh and his girlfriend, and Henry and Margaret. That should be enough excitement."

Josh and Henry were two of the more settled friends of Jack's, and she always enjoyed their company. Jack chose Maxim's, and the six of them arrived around eight o'clock on the evening of Holly's twenty-fifth birthday. The food was exquisite, as usual, and they all laughed and toasted to Holly's good health and prosperity well into the night. The waiter brought a birthday cake, and they all sang to her, much to Holly's chagrin.

Things couldn't have been better, thought Holly as she fixed her make-up in the powder room as they were leaving. They caught a cab, and Jack asked him to wait as he walked her to her door and kissed her goodnight with a hard, long kiss.

"The future certainly looks bright, doesn't it?" Holly's eyes were sparkling.

"You bet," Jack reaffirmed, "Now you get some sleep, tomorrow's a new day."

The months passed, into the fall and then winter line-ups. Holly was busy with the organizing and coordinating of all her departments.

Jack called one day and said, "Don't forget we have to go to the Annual Fashion Awards dinner and seminar in San Francisco next month."

"Oh, I almost forgot about that! I have been so busy with all my buying cutbacks."

Next month rolled around soon enough, and as Holly arrived at the Mark Hopkins Hotel at the top of Nob Hill in San Francisco, she paused to enjoy the magnificent view of the harbor and the Golden Gate Bridge. The sailboats in the harbor looked like tiny white toys as they skipped along, cutting through the whitecaps, across the harbor. She stepped inside the elaborate lobby and checked in at the front desk. The bellman came to take her bags and carry them up to her room on his tall brass cart.

Some of the managers had arrived before her, and Holly greeted them in the hall as she made her way to her room. Holly was well liked by just about all of the managers under her, because of her kind, easy manner. Yet she never for a second let her guard down.

The seminar began with an afternoon of shows and fashion information from the vendors, and there was a discussion period for everyone to raise questions that they had. Then dinner was served and everyone had a prearranged place at one of the fifteen long tables. All were draped with smooth, white damask table-cloths and elaborately set with crystal candlesticks and silver flatware. The flowers in the center of each table were exotic, obviously brought in from Hawaii. The colors were the vivid fuchsia, deep garnet red, golden marigold tones, and set off by wide, flat, shiny green leaves.

All of the department managers were buzzing with chatter about the new fashions, sales figures, and the gossip of each area. Holly went from table to table to greet them all. Some of them she had gotten to know quite well, and some only slightly. Her favorites, naturally, were the ones who had the best sales figures and ran their departments well, not needing pep talks or lectures on incidents gone wrong. Natalie James, who was in Dallas, greeted Holly, genuinely glad to see her. Sitting with Natalie was Christine Harper from the New Orleans store, Gwen Brown from San Diego, and Kristi Duncan, from Los Angeles, whom Holly privately thought was too flashy in her dress and too flirtatious in her manner to truly be considered a professional woman.

Holly chatted with them all for a few minutes, and then returned to her table as the speaker stood up at the main table to speak. He was one of the vice-presidents of Harbinger's, and he congratulated all of the managers on their achievements and sales figures, which were record-breaking in many cases. Then he congratulated Holly on her efforts to secure new and eclectic vendors, raise profit margins, and cut down on returns and markdowns, which was always an area of importance. Holly had been unusually successful in all of these areas by visiting and motivating many of the stores' personnel and scrupulously paring down areas of waste. When he asked Holly to stand and receive the applause, she did graciously, and began her speech.

"I certainly could not have come here today and received such praise and goodwill from you all, if it were not for the many hard-working managers and sales associates all across the area who, each and every day, come to work and give their all. I am very aware of your efforts, and of how self-motivated you have to be to accomplish these figures and record-breaking statistics. It is a competitive world out there, and to succeed you can never let down, or the competition gets one up on you. That is called pressure. Pressure is what drives us, along with desire for achievement, but pressure can take its toll if we do not handle it correctly. No one can take all the credit for him- or herself. I turn to you all and I say 'Thank you'."

Holly continued on and reiterated a few stories of her visits to some of the stores and when she finished, there was a resounding wave of applause, and everyone stood up. Holly saw in Jack's face how proud he was, and it made her happiness even more intensified. After the sumptuous dinner, there was music and some danced, but most stood around talking. Holly went around the room and received congratulations from many of the managers, and chatted at random. She noticed Jack talking to Kristi Duncan, and Kristi was tossing her blonde hair and smiling in her usual flirtatious way.

"When will that girl grow up?" wondered Holly. "She would be so much better off if she made people take her seriously."

Two of the vice presidents came over to talk to Holly and see what her feelings were on the profits of the departments that she was in charge of. There had been such inflated growth over the past three years, and they wanted to keep Harbinger's under control. They were counting on the concentrated efforts of regional managers to stabilize the bottom line. Regional managers reported directly to the vice president of merchandising, and he controlled the buyers.

Holly stayed there talking to the two men for quite some time before one of them noticed that most people had left and gone back to their rooms, as it was close to midnight. Holly was surprised not to see Jack, but figured that he had turned in early, having to do another presentation the next day. She headed for the elevator, happy to end her day. As she was rounding the corner of the corridor on her floor, she caught a glimpse of Jack coming out of the door to one of the other rooms. She was about to speak, but Kristi Duncan stepped out into the hall after him and gave him a hug and languid kiss. She was wearing a very sheer, short robe, and it fell open as she stepped up to embrace him.

Holly stopped short and caught her breath! She stepped back, hidden by the turn of the corner.

She heard him say, "Good night, sweetie, now get your rest for tomorrow, it's going to be busy, and I want you to look your best."

Holly felt a stab at her heart. Her entire chest felt tight, as if she couldn't breathe. "How could he do this?" she asked herself. "I thought he truly cared for me. He's just a playboy, just using women for his entertainment! I thought he had more substance. No wonder he likes his job so much. He gets to travel around and see all of them all the time, and no one knows what's going on."

Holly rushed quickly back to the elevator and stepped into the stairwell across from it to wait while he made his exit on the elevator. It seemed an eternity as he stood there waiting for it to come. Holly listened quietly as she heard the bell signifying that it had arrived on their floor. She heard the doors open and close, and peeked out to see if the coast was clear. He had left, and she continued on toward her own room, feeling as though her world had come unglued.

Holly had a restless night, only able to sleep for a few hours at a time, and then waking up to realize what had transpired. The cold, ice-like grip around her heart kept reminding her of what she had just learned. It was impossible to relax and go back to sleep.

"Well, she thought." This is another example of people letting me down, and I will keep going forward because I have no other choice. This is not going to hurt my life in any way," she resolved.

She woke up the next morning and took an extra-long shower, letting the warm water run over her and relax the tension. She got dressed in an especially beautiful pale green pantsuit with matching leather shoes and purse. As she entered the break-fast-meeting room, Jack saw her and came over to say good morning.

"Hi. I didn't see you last night, you were deep in conversation with Joe Bennett and Jim Barnes. I'm assuming you were solving all of Harbinger's problems."

Holly drew on all of her strength. "Well, yes, we did discuss a lot. After all, this meeting is important to me. I don't have time to fool around."

Holly continued her bright smile and Jack was taken back a moment, but decided that it meant nothing.

"Would you like to sit together?" he asked.

"No. I promised I would sit with some of my managers. They have a few issues that they want to go over," she lied.

"Okay, but I wish we could. I've missed you. You look devastatingly gorgeous today in that shade of green."

"Thank you."

She was barely able to contain herself. Her legs felt like wooden telephone poles as she dragged them over to the table with Natalie, Christine, Gwen, and the devious Kristi. They all were glad to see her and had several questions to ask of her. While she sat there in conversation with them all, Holly observed Kristi and was incredulous to note that she seemed completely comfortable.

Apparently, Kristi felt that her behavior was no big deal and was her normal friendly, outgoing self. Most of the managers knew that Holly was seeing Jack, so Holly decided that Kristi was a good match for Jack, as neither one of them had a conscience, it seemed.

"Well, better that I find out now, rather than later," thought Holly, and that made sense.

The day's agenda was full again with fashion shows from Malaga and Turturro, and a speech from the vice president of operations, Jim Barnes, who used some of the information he had discussed in his conversation with Holly to talk about running the company more efficiently. It was getting toward five o'clock and the seminar was drawing to a close. Holly desperately wanted to leave and not have to face Jack again. She had packed her things before going down to the breakfast meeting, so she walked quickly out at the finish of the meeting and went to the front desk to check out. Upon seeing her, the woman behind the front desk asked if she could send the bellman up for Holly's luggage.

"Oh, that would be great," Holly breathed a sigh of relief. "It would save me so much time."

She quickly signed her account and stepped outside to get a taxi, summoned by the attendant. With her luggage loaded into the cab, Holly headed for the airport and waited to board her plane. Once she was on the plane, she felt in control again. She just wanted to get to her office and get involved in her work again and have as normal a schedule as possible.

She landed in New York and took a cab to her apartment, happy to be home again. As she opened the door to her apartment, she noticed a white note with her name on the front. She opened it, and read: "Welcome back, Holly. Hope you had a successful trip. If you don't mind, I'd like to stop by your office to update about the seminar. I know you're busy, but this might be easier than coming to my office. Thanks, John Morgan."

After she had gotten settled and had things in order at the office, she looked up as her secretary announced that John was coming in. He started, "Holly, I know you're busy, but what happened at the seminar? Did the boys in corporate give out any new info?"

"Not really, but you can tell there is a lot of pressure on the bottom line and the profits for Harbinger's. They just want any input they can get from the front line about merchandising."

"Oh," said John. "Well, you saw Jack, and how is he?"

"There has been a problem," said Holly. "I won't be seeing Jack again."

"What?"

"Apparently, he likes to spread himself around. Doesn't want to be with just one woman. I saw him coming from Kristi Duncan's room late Tuesday night. That's fine with me, if that's what he wants. I just didn't realize it. So now I know," Holly said in a defeated tone.

"I knew that he always was popular with the women, but I thought he had found 'the one' in you, Holly. I'm sorry." John was truly sad from the news.

"I'll be okay. It will take a while, that's all."

"We'll keep you busy around here, Holly. Time will help a lot, you'll see."

"Mr. Morgan, you've always been my staunchest supporter. What would I do without you?" Holly asked.

He gave her a hug, then excused himself and left the bright office to walk the three blocks back to Harbinger's.

Later that day, around four o'clock, Holly's phone rang, and when she picked it up, she knew immediately who it was.

"Hello, darling," Jack said. "I didn't see you before you left. You must have run out in a hurry. What was going on? A crisis back at corporate?"

"No," replied Holly, "I just am very busy, and as a matter of fact, I have been doing a lot of thinking. I feel that my time lately has just been so taken up that I can't even think about having much of a social life. I think that you should begin to date other people and not hold yourself back in any way."

"What are you saying?" asked Jack. "You can't mean this. We mean a great deal to each other, and I won't let you give up on us this way."

"Jack, you have to accept this. I won't change my mind. Please don't call me, I would appreciate it. Good-bye." Holly replaced the receiver and stood up to look out the window toward the skyline.

She called to Mary, her assistant, and said, "Mary, if Jack Navarro calls in the future, please tell him that I am absolutely *not* in. Thank you."

Mary smiled and was secretly happy to hear that. She had never trusted Jack.

Chapter 10
Wind from a Different Direction

For the next four months, Holly worked very hard indeed. There were in-depth reports that she had to make, summer merchandise discounts to oversee, and still the same store visits that she made to keep a close eye on her responsibilities. All this activity helped ease the pain that she still felt over Jack. Every two weeks or so, depending if she were in town, John Morgan would call and ask her to share dinner with him. At first, they would be alone, so she could talk if she wanted to. They would meet at the restaurant around the block from Harbinger's, and have a light dinner. Holly talked a little about it, but really kept most of her feelings to herself. But John knew it helped just to be good company for her.

One evening John brought a friend of his along. Michael Crane was an attorney that John had used both for Harbinger's and for his personal legal matters. Michael was a tall young man with light brown hair, worn rather short, and his clear blue eyes sparkled as he talked. John could see the surprise on her face as they arrived, and he explained that the afternoon appointment he had with Michael had run longer than either of them expected.

"I didn't think you would mind if I brought him along, Holly. I figured he was getting hungry, and I still have to discuss one more problem with him later."

"Of course not, Mr. Morgan," Holly exclaimed. "The more the merrier."

Michael was immediately taken by Holly's beauty, but more important, her easy, gracious ways were so obvious. In New York, this was *not* a trait one saw every day.

"It's nice to meet you, Holly. John has mentioned your name before, so I feel as if I know you." Michael said. "How is your side of Harbinger's doing lately?"

"Quite well, actually. This is such a fast-growing climate for business right now that I want to keep everything in check just in case things change."

"A good idea," remarked Michael. "One can never be too careful."

Then John interjected, "I can't believe how you young people today are so astute, worrying about the future constantly. Why, when I was young we only worried about today and maybe tomorrow."

"The world is different now," Holly replied. "Things change every week."

Michael was so impressed with this bright, easygoing young woman. She was not at all like the fast-paced, pressurized young women of New York that he knew.

They all ordered the same dinner, which was veal parmigiana, one of the specialties of this restaurant. The waiter poured them each a glass of the barolo wine that they chose, and the atmosphere was one of relaxation and good cheer.

Holly thought to herself, "I need to be doing more of this in my life. This is what you call a gentleman. John wouldn't be socializing with him if he were not a good person." They enjoyed their dinners, and talked continually throughout it. Michael was interesting and full of fun. He talked about his law practice, which concentrated on investment fraud. John had been consulting with him for Harbinger's and their need to protect themselves from hostile takeovers.

He also was interested in Holly's career, and seemed fascinated with the way that it had progressed. He genuinely was impressed by the various awards, which she had been presented. When it was over, John and Michael put Holly in a cab for her apartment and headed back to John's office to finish their meeting.

"Let's do this again," Michael said. "I have not enjoyed myself this much for a long time."

After John and Michael had concluded their meeting, John stayed in his office for a while, thinking. Holly seemed to like Michael, and it was obvious to him that Michael thought Holly was great. Sometimes things happen for the best. He had been nervous that she would mind having a stranger there, but it was just the opposite. Maybe now there would be some sunny skies for Holly in her personal life.

John could not help himself the next day. He had to call Holly and see if there was any interest in Michael. "Good morning, Holly. Did you enjoy last night? I am sorry to do that to you, but I had no choice."

"Are you sure you weren't up to something, Mr. Morgan? He surely was nice, and I didn't mind that he came with you."

"Holly, I would never do an underhanded thing to you, you know that. But I got the feeling that you were quite happy with the way things turned out. As a matter of fact, Michael called me earlier and asked more about you. He wanted to know if you were seeing anyone in particular. I told him 'not right now.'"

"Well, isn't that interesting," Holly's voice trailed off.

Two days later, Holly got a phone call at her office. She recognized Michael's voice right away, but pretended that she did not.

"Would you like to get together for dinner tonight or maybe tomorrow night, Holly?"

"Tomorrow would be great," Holly replied, not wanting to seem too eager.

"Super. How about DelVecchio's on Second Avenue? Should I pick you up at your office around 6:30?"

"Fine, I'll be ready."

She couldn't help the flutter that she felt in her stomach. This man seemed to be so very special in so many ways. I'll take it slowly, and keep my eyes wide open, she thought. That way, if I sense anything wrong, I'll just back off.

She made it through the rest of the day and busied herself around her apartment that night.

The next morning, she chose a pretty light blue crepe suit to wear to work, knowing that she would leave from there to go to dinner. She added a pair of pearl earrings and a string of pearls around her neck. She was busy all day and glad of it. The day passed quickly, and before she knew it, it was 5:30, and everyone was leaving. Mary poked her head in the door as she was leaving and asked, "Holly, are you staying late?"

"No, I'm leaving at 6:30. I have an appointment, so I'll close up. Thanks, Mary." Mary knew that meant she had a date. She was glad. She knew how many months it had been since the breakup with Jack, and she thought Holly should get out more.

"Great, see you in the morning, then," called Mary, happily.

Promptly at 6:25, Michael opened the outer door and called, "Anyone home?"

Holly stepped out of her office, and smiled to greet him. "Hello, there. Right on time."

"Oh, yes, I believe in it," Michael replied.

He took her arm and they walked out the door, locking it behind them. On the street they hailed a cab and headed for Second Avenue. DelVecchio's was charming. It had tiny white lights all around the shrubs at the front. Inside, the tables had only small candles, and there was not really any other light in the dining room. It was quite romantic. The candlelight gave a golden glow to Holly's face and lit up her eyes, which looked even greener against the light blue suit.

Michael took a short breath as he noticed how beautiful she looked in the candlelight. "My, you look radiant, tonight," he said. "As though you just came from an exciting adventure."

"Thank you, kind sir," replied Holly, self-consciously.

The dinner was perfect. Holly ordered veal scaloppini, and Michael ordered four-cheese lasagne. He selected a Grand Cru bordeaux, and Holly thought, "He really does have excellent taste in wines."

"Tell me, Holly, what is new with Harbinger's today?"

"Well, I keep hearing rumors of being bought out, and I don't know what to believe. It would be a good investment for some large company, but things are going so well that I hope it can't be true."

"Well, don't worry now. Rumors are always flying, but if I hear anything, certainly I will tell you."

"Okay, then, it's a deal. I won't worry till you tell me to," she laughed.

They talked throughout the dinner and on through cappuccinos and sharing a cannoli.

"It's getting late," Holly said. "I have an early meeting in the morning, and it's around 11:30!"

"Wow! Where did the time go?"

The cab waited as Michael took Holly to her door. He put his arm around her. "Thank you for a wonderful evening, Holly."

He gave her a light kiss on the lips and walked to the elevator. Holly's knees felt weak, and she let herself in and locked the door. Over the next week, Michael took Holly out three more times, and each time they had more fun than the last. Once they invited John Morgan to join them, and he was delighted. He felt that he was at least partly responsible for their happiness.

It was the Christmas rush before Holly realized it, and she had been involved in the holiday promotions and festivities almost every day. Michael's business slowed down a bit around the holidays, but Harbinger's was in full swing. Holly had to work late a lot, and Michael just picked up something and they ate at Holly's place and put their feet up. She didn't have the energy for much more.

After the holidays, it slowed down a bit and Holly could resume a normal pace. She made a quick, three-day visit home to Prairie Ridge in mid-January. All the family was so happy to see her; it had been two years since she had been home. As usual she had gifts for everyone, especially Elizabeth, who had still retained her good looks even though she looked tired.

The youngest of the kids, Clive, was thirteen now, and there were only two at home. Andy had married a girl from the next town and settled down with his own hardware store. Anna was married and had two children. The doctor had advised her not to have more because of her frail health. They all had come to a big dinner when Holly visited and it seemed like Christmas to them all. Jed was fine, but a bit tired after all this time. He enjoyed his rocking chair on the porch more than ever. Holly told her mother about Michael, but tried not to make too much of it, as it was too soon.

"Maybe I'll bring him around in a little while so you can meet him," said Holly.

"That would be great," Elizabeth didn't want to seem eager.

Before she knew it, Holly was back in her office dealing with her everyday issues. Michael called after lunch and welcomed her back. "Did you enjoy seeing your family?" he asked. "I bet they miss you."

"Yes, and I miss them, too. I love to see them, but it is such a different life. I never could have stayed there for any length of time."

"I also grew up in a completely different environment, Holly. I grew up in western Pennsylvania. It was wooded and green, and all my family lived nearby. It was a great way to grow up. I go back every two or three years."

In early April, Jim Barnes, the vice president of operations, called Holly to tell her that the rumors that Harbinger's might be bought out were getting really serious, and he felt she should know.

"It shouldn't make any difference, Holly, if it is Valu-Mart, as they say it is, they will keep the current staff in the same positions. Valu-Mart has lots of money, but they do not have the type of staff to come in and replace ours. They will probably keep us as a money making operation, and let us continue as we are."

"Gosh, I hope so, Jim," Holly said. "I was afraid it might be a competitive chain like Goldberg's, and they would replace our people with theirs."

"We'll just have to ride it out, Holly, and hope for the best," Jim felt optimistic.

Holly called Michael that afternoon and told him about the intended buy-out.

"I just heard about it, too. I was going to call you later." Michael said. "It looks like Valu-Mart is going to make an offer that will do it. They have a lot of money, Holly, and they see Harbinger's as a good investment. Things probably won't change much, but the stock will split and you will have twice the value that you have now!"

"Oh, I never thought about that aspect," she said with excitement.

She was very pleased because her shares of stock had gone up considerably since she took her option to buy them. It was probably worth close to $200,000 now.

The takeover did happen a month later, and all the vice presidents and regional managers were invited to attend an introductory management seminar. The CEO and CFO of Valu-Mart wanted to present their vision for Harbinger's to the senior management staff and enable them to "buy in" to the takeover. It was nicely done, held in Chicago.

The CEO stood up first and welcomed everyone to the team that would be Harbinger's and Valu-Mart. He kept referring to the "team" throughout his speech and emphasized the concept of togetherness and cooperation. He spoke well and everyone listened intently, because their futures were at stake.

When he had completed, the CFO rose and introduced himself. He began his speech by saying, "after all, we must look forward, and do business in a modern kind of way."

He emphasized that there would be no changes at first, and that they expected none. Harbinger's was a highly respected chain, very profitable, and they saw no reason to change that. They felt that personnel were doing a fine job, and unless some unforeseen problem arose, things would remain status quo. Most managers relaxed, but a few were still skeptical. They would be holding monthly meetings for the first six months to facilitate the transition, he announced, and then it would be less frequent. They would also visit the stores as often as possible to become familiar with the day-to-day activities of the stores and get to know the staff. However, the running of the stores would still be left to Harbinger's own corporate staff.

When Holly got back to New York, she immediately called Michael, and they had a lunch discussion about what had transpired. She told him all that was said, and asked, "What do you think of that?"

"Well, I think it is entirely possible that things will go just as they said. However, let's be prepared for something new."

Holly felt better, that Michael's opinion would be more open-minded about the whole thing.

Everything went along as expected for about five months. One day in October, Holly got a phone call from James Cotter, the president of Harbinger's. He had never had that much personal contact with her in the past. She usually dealt with Joe Bennett, the vice president of merchandising, so she was surprised by the call.

"How is everything going, Holly?" he asked. "How are you adjusting to the changes around here?"

"Just fine, Mr. Cotter," Holly replied, wondering what was up.

"Well," he began. "I have some bad news, and some good news for you Holly. Joe Bennett has taken a position with Goldberg's as executive vice president, which is good for him, but we will miss him around here. The good news is that I would like to offer to you the position of vice president of merchandising. Does that sound like something that you would be interested in?"

Holly was speechless for a moment. "Oh, my goodness, Mr. Cotter what an honor, I would be proud to accept the position! When would this take effect?"

"Next week, and of course, you would remain at the same location. Just move upstairs two floors. We'll get together personally and go over the salary and the other fine points."

"Perfect!" replied Holly. "I will begin on Monday, and I'll look forward to seeing you in the near future."

James Cotter hung up the phone and smiled. He felt fortunate to have Holly to move into this position; Joe had surprised him with his notice.

Holly couldn't wait to call Michael and tell him the good news. When she tried his number, his secretary told her that he was in a conference and could not be disturbed.

Holly let out a sigh, and said, "Thanks, Beth, I'll call back in an hour."

Waiting made it seem longer than an hour.

Suddenly, the phone rang, and when she answered it, she heard him say, "What's up?"

"Michael, you won't believe what has happened! I have been offered the VP of merchandising position! Joe Bennett left, and Mr. Cotter just called me."

"I hope you accepted," he replied.

"Of course I accepted! I can't believe it! I start Monday!"

"Let's go out and celebrate tonight, then," Michael asked. "How about DelVecchio's in honor of our first date?"

"Super. Meet you there at seven."

When Holly walked into DelVecchio's there was Michael, sitting at their favorite table with a big bunch of red roses in his lap.

"You are amazing! Where did I ever find you?" Holly asked.

"I'm just proud of you, honey. You deserve that position."

"I have big plans for it," she said. "I have been organizing my agenda and sorting out some ideas."

"Okay, we'll go over them as we eat. I'm famished." They enjoyed their meals, but Holly was so excited that she hardly noticed what it was. She went over with Michael what her ideas were for merchandising and buying and how she could renovate the department. She knew that she had to make a distinct impression when she first went in and do things that were important. Michael helped with some great suggestions, but Holly knew that she had to do these things on her own. They finished up the evening, and he took her home, hating to say good night.

In her office the next day, Holly laid out some new decisions she had been trying to make regarding buying. There seemed to be some great surpluses of merchandise that did not sell, hence it was sold off at tremendous markdowns to consolidators. This caused large amounts of loss of potential profit to Harbinger's. Holly had analyzed the buying statistics for Malaga, Pierre, and Turturro. When she compared one to the other, Malaga had a noticeably higher rate of return and discontinued markdowns than Pierre and Turturro. What this meant was that the merchandise was not selling the way that it should. The Malaga goods bought for all the stores in the chain were being sold off to discounters at twenty percent of the original price. This caused a big loss in the profit margin. Holly had to question the buying of the Malaga Line.

She was sure that the best and most appropriate styles were chosen for Harbinger's. She had always been very selective about the choices and knew that the woman who took over her position when she was promoted didn't make any changes in the way she had always done it. Holly knew that this conclusion meant only one thing: Malaga had to go. It was not appropriate for Harbinger's any longer. She knew that she had to be the one to tell Jack Navarro the bad news. She didn't relish doing it, but it was important to Harbinger's, and it was her job.

She placed a phone call to Jack at his office number. He was not available at the time, so she left a message asking him to call her back, and giving him her new number. In the afternoon of the next day, Jack called and was his usual cheery self on the phone.

"How have you been, Holly?" asked Jack. "I have missed seeing you. You must be very busy."

Holly replied, "Yes, Jack, I am busier than ever, and with my promotion, I can't find enough hours in the day. I wonder if you could come in to see me within the next few days. I have something important to discuss with you."

"Sure." He was certain that she wanted to see him on a personal level. "How about next Wednesday, say about ten o'clock?"

"Fine. See you then." As she hung up, Holly thought, "I sure am glad that I ended that bad situation."

Holly had been feeling anxious for the last twenty-four hours, in anticipation of Jack Navarro's meeting with her and her discomfort in dropping the Malaga Line. He was due in an hour and she was rehearsing what she would say. When ten o'clock arrived, Mary announced that he was here, and showed him in upon Holly's okay.

"Hello," beamed Jack. "It's been a long time. I have been wondering when I'd see you again."

"Hello to you, too," smiled Holly. "What's new in your world?"

"Nothing, really," replied Jack. "To what do I owe this privilege? Oh, and congratulations on your recent promotion. I am sure it was well deserved."

"Thank you," Holly said with a tight smile. "Well, this is business, naturally. Please sit down. I have some news that is going to be difficult. As you know, it is my responsibility to oversee the buying practices and merchandising of Harbinger's. Tied in with these two areas is also profit margins. I have been doing some research lately, and I am sorry to report that the profitability of the Malaga Line is not good at all. It may involve the customer's purchasing decisions lately, or a change in the styles at Malaga, but it is an issue that I cannot ignore. We are under great pressure to control the bottom line of Harbinger's now with the recent takeover, and I have responsibilities that are paramount to me. I am going to have to drop the Malaga Line as of this coming month. I am sorry to tell you this, but I have no choice. All future orders are canceled."

"What?" cried Jack. "How can you say a thing like this to me? Do you realize how large an account Harbinger's is for me? After all we have meant to each other, how can you do this?"

"Of course I realize the size of this account. This is purely a *business* decision. Surely you are aware of the tremendous amount of returns we have had, and I know you realize how much merchandise we have had to give to markdown consolidators. Our personal life has nothing to do with and *will* have nothing to do with dropping the line. This is a decision that I had to make for the future of Harbinger's. I'm sorry."

Jack countered, "We can change the styles, Holly, give me two months. You'll see. I can make it happen."

"Jack, I can't change this now. I have already made the decision, and I have another small line that I think will work. However, if you think that you can make effective changes, then come to me when that has happened. Bring me some samples, sketches, something to work with, and I will take a look at it then. However, for now that is the decision, and I have to stick by it."

"Well, I think that this is a low-down deal, and I'll just get some new designs and turn things around. You'll see." Jack was talking for all he was worth. He wouldn't admit that he had been lazy and unaware of the situation with Harbinger's.

"Fine, I'll wait to hear from you, then." Holly was hoping he'd leave it at that. She was through with this conversation.

"I'll be in touch," he said as he walked out the door.

"Good-bye, Jack." Holly was relieved as he left.

"What a difficult situation," thought Holly. "I would never want to do that again. I'm sure he thinks it was a revenge tactic, but he couldn't be farther from the truth. The fact is, he is lazy and irresponsible about his business, and that did him in." Holly spent the rest of the day going over her reports and revising her figures. She wanted to be very thorough and cover all aspects of her review. Near the end of the day Michael called and asked how her day went.

"Well," she replied. "It went better than I thought it would. However, I felt very uncomfortable, and I'm glad it is over. He definitely thought I was out for revenge. Michael, it's so ridiculous, he doesn't even realize that he had completely lost track of his business. He is so busy taking time off and playing around that he lost control."

"You can't worry about that now, you have done all that you can. It is out of your hands, and that's the end of it." Michael spoke firmly.

"Let's go to dinner, I want to relax now."

"Fine. Where shall we go?"

"Let's go to that new little Italian place down on Houston Street. They have a great lobster fra diavolo." Holly suggested.

"Fine by me. You know I love lobster."

They were there in fifteen minutes. As they entered the restaurant, they noticed a woman sitting at the front table. She spoke to Holly, and it took Holly a minute to recognize her.

"Peggy!" said Holly. "What a surprise. I didn't know you were still in this area."

"I'm not," said Peggy. "I am here tonight with my fiancée, Richard Stevens, please say hello to him. Richard, this is Holly Cummings, an old friend and former manager of mine from Harbinger's."

"Nice to meet you, Richard. This is my friend Michael Crane. Michael, meet Peggy Newcomb and Richard Stevens."

"My pleasure. What brings you to this area?"

"Well," Peggy began. "I had left and gone to White Plains to work. It is such busy area now. I got a job as manager of a store in a medium-sized chain out of Boston. It is called Casual Living. They specialize in active wear. It has been good for me, and now I am regional manager for the Northeast area. Richard and I met through business, and it is a short story from there."

As she spoke, Peggy was edging her way to the side, and within a few moments she and Holly were just far enough back from Richard and Michael that they could have their own conversation. Michael and Richard kept talking, and soon they were discussing sports.

Peggy started, "Holly, I can't tell you how bitter I was when I was let go from Harbinger's. I didn't realize what I had done, and I had a hard time getting myself back on track. I felt sorry for myself, and I kept making excuses for my bad behavior. Can you ever forgive me? After a while, I began to see just what I had done to you and also to myself, and how I would feel if someone ever did that to me. So I turned myself around, and that is when I started to really progress and get promotions. I owe it all to you."

"Nonsense. Everyone is entitled to a mistake. I certainly don't feel any ill will. I am so happy to hear that you are doing well. Mr. Morgan is as great as ever, and I see him frequently, even though I don't work near him any more."

"What exactly do you do now?" asked Peggy.

"I am vice president of merchandising, and loving every minute of it."

"Super!" cried Peggy. "Good for you. I bet you're doing a great job."

Just then Richard came over, "Peggy, we had better go. We'll be late for the show."

"Well, bye, now. Hope we can meet again."

Holly bade her friend good-bye and they left.

"Is she from the distant past?" asked Michael.

"It's a long story. I'll tell you about it some day. But I feel better knowing that things are comfortable between us, and that she is doing well. Let's get a table. I'm famished."

As they sat enjoying their lobster fra diavolo, they spoke only rarely. The food was delicious, and they were so tired from the day's activities that they just ate quietly.

"I would love this recipe," said Michael. "I'm trying to guess what the seasonings are, so we can try to duplicate it. When the waiter comes, I'm going to ask him a few questions."

They shared a carafe of pinot grigio, and as they drank the last glasses of it, the waiter appeared.

"Tell me. What is it that makes this sauce on the lobster so special?"

"The secret is just that it takes four and a half to five hours to make this sauce," he replied. "You can't hurry it. You know when you eat Italian food, you have to go by the rules and regulations. People come in here and they say they want to order food but make changes, or add cheese to something that shouldn't have cheese. You can't do that. One more thing: Don't ever put sugar in your sauce. That's caramelizing it. I tell them Italy is an old country, we have been making this food for a long time and you can't come and tell us how to change it to suit Irish or English or Polish tastes. You have to follow the rules and regulations. That's the way it is."

When the waiter left, Michael and Holly laughed and finished their glasses of wine, ready to call it a day.

"What a great evening," Holly murmured, "a great finish to a difficult day."

A week later Holly got a phone call from James Cotter. He asked Holly if the following Tuesday were convenient for her to meet with him.

"Certainly, Mr. Cotter. What time is good?"

"Why don't you come over here at ten, right after the weekly meeting that I have on Tuesdays?"

"Great." She confirmed.

When Tuesday arrived, Holly was anxious. Now was the time to negotiate her salary, and she wanted to get the best possible. She had gone over strategies with Michael quite a bit, and felt that she was comfortable with the issues. As she walked into the foyer of James Cotter's elegant office, she spoke to the receptionist, Sheila. She offered her a seat on one of the silk settees in the front area. Sheila phoned Mr. Cotter's assistant, and was told to send Holly right in.

As she approached the assistant, she said, "Hello, Kim, how are things today?"

Kim knew her response was to be an indication toward James Cotter's mind-set, and she replied, "Things seem to be going well, Holly. I think this is going to be a good day, have a seat, please."

With that information, Holly relaxed just a tiny bit. Kim had worked for James Cotter for fifteen years, and she and Holly knew each other from coming up through the ranks. They had a mutual respect for each other.

Holly entered Cotter's office, and he greeted her with a firm handshake and big smile. "How are you, Holly? I have been looking forward to seeing you. Have a seat, please. Would you like a cup of coffee?"

"Thank you, no, I have had enough today. It's good to see you, also, Mr. Cotter."

Mr. Cotter began, "The Columbus holiday sale had great traffic, and it looks like we are going to come in five percent above plan. The only place where we had a little problem was in the Florida stores, where we had a tropical storm, and that hurt business in the Miami and Ft. Lauderdale stores. Now, I know that this is a little like 'the cart before the horse,' but I wanted to wait to negotiate your salary a little because I knew you would have some renovations and changes to offer once you were put into your new position. That is more ammunition that I have, to negotiate a good salary for you with the Valu-Mart people. I have to get the okay from them and justify every penny to them."

"I understand," replied Holly, "and I have prepared some recommendations that I wanted to present to you and also the Valu-Mart board."

Holly handed a twenty-page report to Cotter, and he took about ten minutes to read it over. During that time, Holly thumbed through a company newsletter that was on his coffee table. It told of some social gatherings within the company and promotions and retirements that had transpired over the last two months.

After he had read the report, he smiled, and said. "This is super. Some of these observations are excellent, and I feel we can really use some of these cost-cutting suggestions right away. Now, let's get down to the salary issue. I am prepared to give you a twenty percent raise, and along with that is the news that the stock has split once again, so your shares are worth double what they were last week, and an option for five hundred more shares. I think that these two facts should make your financial future look quite bright. What do you say?"

"Well, I feel that this is certainly good news about the stock split. Also, I am grateful for the raise. I know that Valu-Mart had said that we will run ourselves, but I also know that they oversee everything and monitor Harbinger's decisions as well. However, I feel that in light of the plan that I have presented, I don't think that the pay increase is enough. I would rather have my compensation linked to my performance."

"How do you propose that we do this?" he questioned.

Holly spent the next thirty minutes explaining how her sales plan for each quarter's sales figures would tie in directly to an end-of-the-year bonus plan. She expected if things went her way, she would earn quite a bit more than the twenty percent raise.

Cotter had to admit that her plan had merit; if the profitability of the company went up, then she would be compensated for it. If it did not, then she would not earn a raise. She would be motivated to see that the company was profitable. If the company was profitable, it could afford to pay her. Also, her year-end bonuses would be paid at a time that would help the company tax-wise. He agreed to the plan, and they said good-bye. Holly walked out the door into the front reception area and said good-bye to both Kim and Sheila. She gave Kim a thumbs-up sign to let her know everything went well. Kim smiled.

When she reached her own office by cab, Holly was feeling very satisfied. "Now," she muttered to herself. "I have my work cut out for me." She reread a copy of her plan and made even more revisions to it in pencil. Around three o'clock, Michael called to see how the compensation meeting had gone.

"It went beautifully. Now all I have to do is follow through!"

"You will. You always do."

After she hung up with Michael, Holly called each of her regional managers and told them she was going to have a meeting on Monday there at corporate headquarters, at ten o'clock. She knew that they had to understand and buy into it, so that it would be as successful as possible. Each of them seemed eager to come to corporate and tighten up the merchandising strategy.

The week passed quickly, and before she knew it, Monday rolled around. The first to arrive was Jane Marks, the Eastern Regional merchandising manager. Then in came Connie Jordan, Southern regional manager and with her was Sally Benson, Western regional manager. The last to arrive was John McCormick, the Northern regional manager. They all joined Holly in her large office and pulled up chairs at her huge glass and mahogany conference table by the window, overlooking Central Park. Mary, her assistant, brought carafes of coffee and a platter of pastries and set them in the middle of the table.

Holly started the meeting by saying, "All of you have been doing a fantastic job and there is nothing that I could complain about. However, now that we are well into the buyout, and Valu-

Mart is no longer treating us like the new kid on the block, we also won't get a break. Corporate is still in charge of what we do, but you can bet everything you have that Valu-Mart is watching every move and getting reports on all the figures. We have to make sure that this quarter is one of our best, and keep them happy that they made the investment in us.

"There are several ways that we can ensure that this happens. I have revamped the program for surpluses, returns, and discontinued styles, as you can see on these reports. I also have made changes in some of our buying strategies. That is all outlined on pages eight, nine, and ten. I have taken on a new small but exclusive vendor from Italy, and I think it will be very successful. Maybe some of you have seen the samples, which arrived at the stores last Thursday and Friday. They are dynamite, and I urge you to go to each of your stores and give motivation seminars to all managers and sales associates. This should ensure good sales figures to start off with. Soon the holiday season begins, and that will give us the opportunity to end the year with strong figures. Does anyone have any suggestions, changes, or ideas to share?"

A few questions were raised, ideas to strengthen the figures for the last quarter of the year talked about, and then they all were quiet.

Holly spoke again. "I know you all are capable of tremendous effort and impressive figures. So I urge you to take these reports, read them carefully, and put the ideas to use so we all can benefit from the strong ending we are going to have this year. Now, we are all going to go to lunch and relax."

They left the office together and headed for a little French lunchroom down the block. During lunch, a little business conversation ensued, but they mostly ate and relaxed and appreciated their new boss's generous attitudes.

Chapter 11
Legal Tradewinds

Michael had spoken to Holly later in the day, and she informed him how everything went in the meeting. He admired Holly's skill with people, and he knew that she would accomplish her goals because she knew how to motivate and communicate with people to obtain her goals.

Michael's own career in law was progressing nicely, and he hoped it would grow as he had planned. He had made partner after four years at his law firm, Carter, Sprague and Hutchinson, a good-sized firm. He wanted dearly, though, to land a really large or important case to make his mark. A couple of the new attorneys had landed good cases and he felt that it was time for him to do so. He had been working on obtaining the Piedmont case, which was a case of a takeover and fraudulent information about the Lothrup Company, a medium-sized textile manufacturing company which was in Chapter 11, trying to get out from under huge debt and overextended operating costs.

The Piedmont Mills company had been able to take it over to try to turn the business around. Lothrup hired a defense attorney to protect them from liability in a suit filed by Piedmont for giving fraudulent information prior to the takeover. Every day in the papers there was an article about it, and the public was following the story closely. The textile industry was going through a great change, and everyone wanted the mills, located along the rivers, to remain. Pollution was decreasing, and no one wanted the Far East to take the business away from American mills. Jobs would be lost, families would have to move away, and there was strong public opinion. Michael was one of the best prosecuting attorneys in fraud cases, and there was only one other strong contender for the position.

Milkweed

Timothy Willoughby III was the son of a partner in one of the oldest law firms in New York. His grandfather had started the firm in 1915. Willoughby and Barnett was well known and well connected politically. Timothy, himself was a bit of a slacker, though he was bright. Timothy felt "why work hard when you don't have to?" The most prominent judge in the area, Judge James Parker, had known Timothy's father since they attended law school together at Harvard. Michael felt that his chances of getting the case were hurt by this friendship.

Usually, Judge Parker would offer some polite conversation to Michael and change the subject. He had seen Michael in court quite a few times over the years, and he had admired his intelligence and ability to talk to a jury. The decision on representation was approximately two weeks away, and Michael had been quite preoccupied. He knew it wasn't the end of the world if he didn't get the case, but he knew he would do the best job, and there would be others if he didn't get it.

Timothy Willoughby III had been drinking since lunchtime that Wednesday afternoon when he had met an old college pal at the Blue Swallow Bar on 46th Street. Timothy liked to go to the Blue Swallow because no one of any importance would see him there, and also because it was next door to the Kitty Kat Klub. Often the girls would come in before they went in to dance at the Klub. Timothy liked to talk and sit with the girls because he felt shy around women in general. They always seemed to have clever things to say, and he didn't. He envied other men who went right up to girls and started an easy conversation.

This particular day, Timothy was sitting at the bar, having a sandwich and a few scotch and sodas. Before he had finished his sandwich, Harry Douglas came up to him and recognized him from Superior Law School where they had both graduated from. Timothy couldn't get into Harvard because of bad grades and a lax attitude, even with his father as an alumnus. Harry sat down with Timothy and they proceeded to drink some scotches together.

At about seven o'clock, two dancers from the Kitty Kat Klub came in and sat next to Harry and Timothy. They started to talk to the two men and were having some laughs, when a tough, unshaven man in a flannel shirt and jeans walked over to them.

"What do you two jokers think you're doing with my girls?" said the man. "They don't want to talk to you."

The girls started to object, but the man interrupted. "Don't try to make this look okay, girls. I know you don't want to be talking to these two losers."

"What?" cried Timothy. "These girls are my friends, and they want to spend time with me and my buddy here. Mind your own business."

The man jumped forward to grab Timothy, and Harry took a swing and hit him square in the face. Blood started to drip out of his nose. Then Timothy stepped to the side and missed a punch that the stranger threw at him. Timothy was mad, now. After all, he really wanted to talk to these women, and he didn't want to look bad in front of them. Now he took a swing, and he connected with the man, sending him crashing into the wall of glasses that were piled up behind the bar.

Glass was everywhere, and people started to scream. The man got up from the floor, and punched Timothy hard in the stomach and threw him on top of a table, breaking it in three pieces. Then two other men joined in the melee, and more glasses and chairs were smashed. The bartender dialed the police, and they arrived in four minutes.

The police stormed in the front door and grabbed Timothy and Harry, then slammed them up against the bar, handcuffing them all in one motion. Two more policemen came in and handcuffed the stranger and three other men who had been knocked unconscious on the floor. A reporter for the *New York Sun* walked in and snapped photos of everything he could see.

Timothy had bail made for him by midnight, and was home by one in the morning, but his picture was on the lower part of the front page of the newspaper the next morning. The description of the barroom brawl and the dancers from the Kitty Kat

Klub was not exactly what his father had wanted his son to be involved in.

When Michael read the morning paper, he dropped his jaw in surprise. He quickly realized what this meant to his pursuit of the Piedmont case. On the other side of Central Park, Timothy Willoughby Jr. also realized what this meant as far as the choice of an attorney in the Piedmont case. He knew this was very bad press for his son.

"You stupid idiot!" He roared to his son on the phone. "What were you doing at that cheap bar again? I thought you told me you wouldn't go there any more. Look at your picture all over the front page!"

"How was I to know, Dad? I figured no one would know. I didn't see any photographer." whined Timothy III.

Judge Parker also read the paper Thursday morning.

Michael received a call from the CEO of Piedmont Friday morning around ten informing him that he had been awarded the case, if he wanted it, and he should start preparations. They would go to trial in three months.

Preparing for trial was most important, as it would show fraudulent misrepresentation about the financial situation of Lothrup. Michael had to uncover information to prove that Lothrup overstated their profits by reducing the cost of goods sold. Someone tampered with this. "This was an inside job," he thought. "I had better get to the bottom of this." Michael had a copy of what was on file with him, and when he put them side by side, you could see how the figures were changed. When Piedmont took over Lothrup, they thought that they were making a better deal than they actually did.

In running Lothrup for the first few months, Piedmont felt they were in good shape. Upon comparing the figures as they got into the next few months, the accountants discovered the altered figures—purchases that were never recorded as cost of goods sold.

That afternoon, Michael went down to the corporate offices of Lothrup. He knew that he was not welcome there, being the prosecuting attorney, so he gave an alias to the receptionist at the front desk. He gave the name of the person that he was going to see as Jonathan Litton, a young corporate attorney, with whom he had struck a friendship because of a New York Bar Association committee they both were on.

Jonathan was pleased to see Michael, even though he knew Michael's position now as prosecuting attorney.

"Hi, Jonathan," Michael greeted his friend. "How is it going here at Lothrup?"

"It's okay. Nice to see you, Michael. I have a couple of irons in the fire, and I hope it won't be too long before I hear something." Jonathan didn't plan on staying at Lothrup much longer, with all the gossip about the fraudulent figures and financial situation.

"I wonder if you can give me any small bit of information about the financial department of Lothrup, so I can figure who could have altered those figures. I know it was an inside job. Is there anyone that you think might have been able to be corrupted?" Michael needed information from his friend.

Jonathan replied, "There are only two people that would have had access to those financials. They are John Waters, VP of finance, and Ed Hughes, the CPA whom we use. I see a dead end."

"Okay. I appreciate your help. Let me know if I can do anything for you in your next move. I'd be happy to do whatever I can."

"I know you would, buddy. Thanks," Jonathan bade him good-bye.

Michael went back to his office and thought about what had transpired. He knew he had to find the weak link in the financial department of Lothrup. He made a few phone calls to associates and asked questions about John Waters. Even though New York was a big city, it was like a small town when people were doing things that were questionable.

He was given information that although John Waters was a capable VP of finance, he had one weakness that was serious: an obsession of betting at the racetrack. Apparently, he was wrong a lot more often than he was right in picking his horses. He was into his bookie for about $400,000, and it was long overdue. "Now, if that isn't an opportunity to be pressured to do something that you shouldn't, I don't know what is," thought Michael. "What an easy way to get out of financial problems and pay off his debts."

Apparently, the bookie and some of his family had stock in Lothrup, and with the takeover, they were expecting their stocks to go up. Quickly realizing the connection to Lothrup, the bookie pressured Waters to alter the figures, offering to forgive the debt.

After having spent five hours straight on this scenario, Michael decided to call it a day. He telephoned Holly, and she was happy to hear about what was going on with the case. It had been a great mystery to her also. After all, this had a great deal of bearing on Michael's career.

When she heard his voice, Holly felt a rush of excitement. "Tell me, what's new," she pleaded.

"Well, not much. Only that I now know what happened and who did it!"

"No! Who was it that altered the figures?"

"Apparently the VP of finance, John Waters," Michael replied. "Now I have to prove this in court."

"I can't believe that you actually got to the bottom of this and figured it out so easily."

"Well, it wasn't so easy," Michael reported. "It took some hard thinking and some snooping around, which I'm good at."

"You certainly are," she agreed. "Now, show me how good you are at proving it in court! Let's go over to DelVecchio's and celebrate your breakthrough."

"Fine. I'm famished."

When they arrived at DelVecchio's, the owner greeted them at the door.

"Good evening, my friends. How are you both tonight?"

"Just fine." Michael answered. "We have had quite a day."

The trial began two months later in January, and Michael felt he had adequate time to get everything together. He had all the altered documents, and he also had subpoenaed John Waters to testify about the changes made in the financials. The trial progressed along normally with the documents being examined by the judge. The members of the jury were each given a chance to make a close examination of the documents. The documents were viewed on a large screen in the courtroom for all to see. There was no question that they had been altered.

Michael was afraid that he would have to rely on technical information about the fraudulent figures if Waters's testimony didn't go well. However, a deal was struck with Waters, and he testified completely, giving all necessary information about the blackmail against him, and why it transpired. He got off with a five-year sentence, and two years of that sentence were suspended.

Michael was ecstatic at the verdict and felt that the sentence given to Waters was fair. It was the trial of the year for New Yorkers, and Michael's name was being spoken in all the best places. Holly was very proud of his accomplishments and felt that winds of good fortune were blowing through their lives.

Chapter 12
Storm Brewing

The month was March, and much of Holly's busy time with the holidays and New Year's business had quieted down. She was thinking about visiting home again, as she missed her family and had not seen them for over a year. She asked Michael if he would like to join her in visiting the family. He replied that he would like to, but it was still busy for him, and he would do it another time.

This was difficult for Holly to accept, as it took some time for her to decide to ask him to come. She was afraid he would find it such a different world. Perhaps he might not feel comfortable, perhaps he might not understand them, perhaps he might not like them; all these thoughts ran through her head. When he declined the invitation, she began to have doubts.

Holly felt that Michael had become wrapped up in his law career and perhaps their personal lives would suffer in the meantime.

She brought this up with him. "I really wish that you might be able to get away for just a few days to come with me, Michael. The family would like to meet you and there is so much for you to know about each one of them. I know that your case is through and you really don't have any more obligations with that any more."

"I just don't have time right now. I need a break to get my mind back on track after so much time with this case taking over my life. I need to be here in my office, getting things in place."

Holly gave in, but still felt disappointment. She planned her trip for a full week to allow her to visit all the members of her family. She flew out of Newark airport, changed planes in Charlotte, North Carolina, and then went on to Columbia. Clive picked her up at the airport, and hugged her tight when she came down the stairway.

"Gosh, Holly, you get prettier every year. I can't believe it."

"Oh, Clive, you just plain love me too much." Holly exclaimed.

After a big family get-together and meal that wouldn't stop, Holly sat back in one of the rocking chairs on the front porch and just took everything in. She missed the sweet, warm winds; the easy, slow ways; and the simple family attitudes that they all enjoyed.

She looked out on the fields across the dirt road and saw the graceful milkweed plants blowing in the spring breezes and smiled. "Those milkweed plants," she thought. "They just keep growing, no matter what. If there is a drought, they survive. If there is a storm, they hang tight. If there is cold, they brace themselves."

Holly got up and walked out onto the road and began to amble along aimlessly. She kicked at a stone as she wandered, and diligently kept it on an even course in front of her. She had been good at keeping her life on track; her business career had gone along well. She had her ups and downs, like anyone else. That was to be expected; no one had all successes. It was only through the mistakes that one really learned important lessons in life. She had enjoyed them all. She wouldn't have had it any other way.

But now she felt that it was going astray. She had really planned on a future with Michael. However, she had this feeling that things were falling away. Now she had to keep her personal life on track, not allow it to take a side road.

Just then, Jed caught up with her. "Holly, wait up for yer' ol' Pa. I want to walk a bit with my girl."

"Sure, Pa, I'd love to walk a bit with you."

"How is everythin' goin' for ya, Holly? You seem a bit quiet, and that ain't like ya. I know ya talked 'bout this Michael comin'. Now he ain't here. Did somethin' happen? Tell yer ol' Pa."

Holly hesitated. "Well, I just feel that things are different. Michael has had a great success lately, and he seems distant and different to me."

"Well, girl," Pa said. "Things are always different, Holly. Whenever things change, people change. The trick is to change along with them, too. Maybe he has a lot on his mind. Maybe he has troubles you don't know about. Give him time and he'll tell you 'bout it. I always say, 'never do nothin' in a hurry'."

"I guess you're right, as usual. I should relax and see what happens. It can't be that bad. I'm just uptight," Holly said gratefully.

Somehow in his simple wisdom, Pa saw the reality in things and it gave her great security.

"The main thing is that I have a good visit with everyone, and spend time with those I love. Tomorrow I'm spending the day with Anna and her family."

The two Cummingses continued walking down the dirt road, with their arms around each other's shoulders, as the soft pink sunset sank below the line of thick green trees on the horizon.

The next morning, Holly awoke and quickly got dressed to spend the day with her twin and her two children. She ate a light breakfast of baking powder biscuits and honey with a strong cup of coffee, brewed in the tinware pot that Ma had owned for thirty years. The pot was dark blue with a white spatter pattern on it. There were a few dents in it, but it brewed the best coffee that Holly had ever tasted and always would. She sat at the handmade wooden table that her father had constructed thirty-five years ago when he and Elizabeth had first built their home for their soon-to-be family. What happy times this room had witnessed; what change and growth that the family had gone through! Whenever she came to visit, Holly would enjoy sitting in the front room and soak up the atmosphere that was felt there. It always rejuvenated her and gave her an appreciation of life.

Holly went in the horse-drawn wagon with Clive over to the other side of town to visit Anna. She lived with her husband, Ted, and two children, Alice and Benjamin. They were happy to have her come to see their home. Ted was an amiable man, who was in partnership with Andy in the hardware store. They now had two hardware stores, one in Prairie Ridge and the other in Glen Fork, ten miles to the north. Anna welcomed Holly into the house and called to the children to come out and see their aunt. Alice came out first and gave Holly a hug. Holly was surprised to see how much her niece resembled Elizabeth. Alice was soft-spoken with blonde hair and bright blue eyes. Then out came Ben, who was tall with darker hair, like his father, and dark eyes. Ben also gave Holly a hug and told her how happy he was to see her again. They both heard stories regularly about their aunt and her life in New York.

They all sat in the living room and had cookies and home-made lemonade. Alice and Ben were so comfortable talking about their activities in school and friends that Holly felt a slight pang that she did not have her own family to share daily events with, and be with at the end of each day. Anna seemed to be healthy. Holly had always worried about this and kept in constant touch with her to be sure that she was doing well. Anna helped out in the hardware store in Prairie Ridge sometimes and that allowed Andy or Ted to spend more time at the Glen Fork store. Anna had valued her experience at the general store when Holly left for New York because that helped her to be useful to her husband when he and Andy opened up their store in Prairie Ridge. Clive stayed to visit for a while, enjoying the comfortable conversation that took place.

However, after about an hour he said that he had to get back to the farm to do some chores for Pa. He was the only one remaining on the farm, and Jed and Elizabeth relied on him a lot. The cotton crop had been cut way back and most of the extra acreage was leased out to farmers without their own land to grow crops on, who then paid a percentage to Jed and Elizabeth at the end of the growing season.

Ted came in to join the group after about two hours. He knew Holly was coming and didn't want to lose out on the visit. Ted was close to all the family, being partners with Andy and having joined the family when he married Anna.

Andy came in after the store closed at 5:30, and joined in on the hearty conversation and kidding that took place. He was glad to see his sister and wanted to spend as much time with her as he could. Andy had three children of his own now, and he loved hearing from his sister in the big city. He had often wondered what would have happened if she had been able to get some type of job for him in New York.

They reminisced after dinner until around 8:30, and then Clive came in the wagon to get Holly and take her back to the homestead. When she returned to her parent's home, they were sitting on the front porch in the rocking chairs, talking and sipping lemonade. Elizabeth asked Holly to join them and just relax a little as it grew dark.

"Tell me, Holly," Elizabeth began. "What's new with you and Michael? I remembered that ya' said ya' was a bringin' him to visit soon."

Elizabeth was fishing, wanting to know just what her daughter's future was bringing.

"Well, Ma," Holly answered. "Michael has been busy with a very important case. Now he needs time to get reorganized. I'll bring him just as soon as I can. Don't you worry."

Holly knew that her Pa had discussed this with her mother, and Elizabeth wanted to form her own opinion. Holly had told them about Michael for quite some time now, and they were anxious to meet this man that Holly seemed to hold in such high esteem.

Three days of her visit had passed, and Holly was really relaxing, but she couldn't help thinking of Michael and how he was doing back in New York.

Chapter 13
Nature Takes Over

Michael had awakened early the next morning and had a feeling of being completely out of sorts. He couldn't figure what it was, but he knew he needed to see Holly. "I really was overreacting to the idea of going with her to visit the family," he thought. "What a mistake. I really didn't need more than a couple of days to get myself squared away and ready for the next round of events. I am missing a great opportunity, and I don't want to let it get away. Holly's family is so important to her, and I want to get to know them as soon as I can."

Michael called an airline and arranged to take a flight arriving in Columbia at four o'clock that day. Then he had called the house to let them know he was coming while Holly was out doing an errand with Clive and made Elizabeth and Jed promise not to tell her. They were all out on the front porch again rocking and chatting when Andy drove up in his truck and let a passenger out in front of the house. Holly squinted her eyes, let out a gasp, and jumped down to run to the front gate.

"Michael!" she cried. "What are you doing here? How did you find the place? Andy, what's going on? Did all of you know about this?"

"Calm down, Holly! I decided that I had better get down here before I regretted it for the rest of my life."

He took her in his arms and gave her a long, hard kiss on the lips. All of the Cummings clan cheered as they stepped apart and headed for the front porch to sit and rock, giving everyone a chance to meet Michael.

The entire family sat out on the porch that night until almost midnight. There was so much to talk about, so many questions to ask Michael. He found them all to be most exceptional, reminding him of his own family in Pennsylvania, and he fit right in easily. After the last of them had gone to bed or left for their own home, Holly and Michael wandered down the dirt road, hand in hand.

"Holly," Michael began, "you and I have dedicated enough time to our careers, each of us has achieved what I think we wanted to. Now I think it's time that we dedicate time to our personal lives. We need to make a commitment to our future and a family of our own. I want to marry you, Holly. What do you say?"

"Michael," Holly replied with a tear in her eye, "I thought you'd never ask!"

As they walked back toward the little homestead, Holly watched the milkweed plants in the moonlight, bending gracefully in the spring breeze—still strong, and still surviving.

DATE DUE
